'I'm there when it gets dark, to kill you if I can . . .'
The Bogey Man's sinister but compelling chant used to scare
the wits out of Gary Scott when he was a five-year-old, growing
up in the worst part of Glasgow. But now, nearly twenty years
later, he's an experienced and, he likes to think, hard-nosed
magazine editor. He's far too preoccupied with real life in all
its seedy variety to bother with imaginary horrors. So why
does he keep being drawn back to the dark closes and
crumbling tower blocks of Maryhill?
As one increasingly bizarre and grisly event succeeds another,
as the deaths begin to pile up, Gary realises that he himself is,
somehow, inextricably involved. Then, one night, the Bogey
Man arrives under his window . . .
*Of Darkness and Light*, Barry Graham's first novel, is an
elegant story of horror both physical and psychological, a taut
and vivid slide into panic, set in a Glasgow whose darker side is
brilliantly rendered. Shirley Girdwood's broodingly suggestive
drawings complement the text perfectly. This is an impressive
debut.

First published in Great Britain 1989

This paperback edition published 1990

Text copyright © 1989 Barry Graham

Illustration copyright © 1989 Shirley Girdwood

Bloomsbury Publishing Ltd, 2 Soho Square, London W1V 5DE

A CIP catalogue record for this book is available from the British Library

ISBN 0–7475–0677–9

10 9 8 7 6 5 4 3 2 1

Typeset by Bookworm Typesetting, Manchester
Printed and bound in Great Britain by Cox and Wyman, Reading, Berkshire

# OF DARKNESS

## AND

# LIGHT

BARRY GRAHAM

Illustrated by Shirley Girdwood

BLOOMSBURY

# Foreword

While Maryhill is a real place, there is no such place as
Hunterdunn Street, and all the characters and events
described in this novel are the product of my imagination.
I'd like to thank my friend Sergio Casci for his constant
advice, criticism and encouragement. Thanks are also due to
Shirley Girdwood, for liking it, and to Galya for helping keep
things rolling.

Barry Graham

**FOR SERGIO CASCI**

# ONE

It's half-five now, half-five in the morning. It's daylight. This being early July – the third, I think – it'll probably start getting dark sometime between ten and eleven tonight. If I keep at it all day, that gives me about sixteen hours, including tea and toilet breaks. Not very much, considering what I have to do.

Sixteen hours to tell you about Rhona and Peter and Trish and me and that other. And you probably won't believe a word of it if you read it. Not that I give a shit; not that I'll be around to give a shit. I hope you'd be right not to believe me. I hope I'm full of shit. I hope you're not reading this, because if you are, I was right.

When I finish this, I'll post it to Ian at the mag. But I'd better finish it first, hadn't I?

All right.

Where to start? I could go back further, but if I'm going to describe what happened in enough detail, I'd better start with a Monday morning not that long ago. Trish hadn't stirred when her radio alarm-clock came on at six-thirty. Normally a heavy sleeper, I woke at once. I sat up in bed, switched off the radio on the bedside table and lay down again.

Trish sighed in her sleep and snuggled against me. I kissed her very lightly on the temple. With her red hair tousled on the pillow and her face sullen in sleep, she looked closer to five years old than twenty-five. As she pressed against me, I was tempted to wake her up for an early-morning fuck. Although my erection put up a strong argument in favour, I decided against it. She'd been up late; better to let her sleep.

As I gently disengaged myself from her arms and got out of bed, Trish muttered, gave a little snort and settled down again. Naked, I went to the bathroom and relieved myself, then went back to the bedroom to dress. I was pulling my T-shirt over my scrawny shoulders when Trish sat up in bed. She smiled at me drowsily. 'You're up early,' she said, blinking.

'Mm. Didn't sleep too well,' I answered, fastening my trousers.

'Are you going now, or do you want some breakfast?' she asked.

'Yeah, I'm hungry. I wouldn't mind.'

'Good – you know where the kitchen is,' she smirked. 'I'll have some muesli while you're there.'

I went over to the bed, slid my hand under the quilt and seized her ankle. 'Somebody's feet are about to get tickled . . .'

'Gary! Don't! *Gary!*' she shrieked. 'Don't you dare! *I'll kill you!*' Gently, I tickled the sole of her foot. The result was similar to an epileptic fit. 'You pig! Stop it!' she screeched.

'Ask me nicely and I'll think about it.'

2

She lunged at me, threw her arms around my neck and began to cover my face with light kisses. I let go of her foot and she lay back, kissing me long and deeply as she pulled me down on top of her. 'Was that nice enough?' she asked softly.

'That'll do.' I kissed her hungrily. My appetite for breakfast had mysteriously disappeared. I began to undo my belt.

Trish affected an air of wide-eyed innocence. 'What're you doing?'

'I'll show you.' And I did.

An hour later, I was on the verge of falling asleep when she gave me a nudge. 'D'you want some breakfast now?'

I looked at the clock. 'Nah. I'd better get going. Work to be done.'

'Work?' She looked surprised. 'That doesn't sound like you.'

'I know, I know.' I grinned at her sarcasm. 'But it's my time of the month. The mag won't produce itself.'

'Will I see you tonight?'

'Don't think so,' I said. 'I want to get some more of my play written.'

'We *are* being conscientious, aren't we?'

'Not through choice. If I don't give it to them soon, the BBC're liable to lose interest.'

'How much have you done so far? Is the title finished yet?'

'Laugh it up, Philistine.' I got out of bed and began to dress. 'They laughed at Beckett too.'

'Sorry, Samuel.' She stretched, then got up. I had to

3

look away from her, or the sight of her soft, lazy nakedness would've made sure we were both late for work. 'Are you having a shower, smelly?'

'No, I don't have time.'

'Well, I'm having one now.' She went out of the room.

I finished dressing and combed my hair. I was about to leave when I heard Trish call my name from the bathroom. I went through and opened the door, to be met by a cloud of steam. Trish was standing under a very hot spray, shampooing her red curls. 'When'll I see you next?' she asked.

My glasses had steamed up. I took them off and wiped them on my jumper. 'How about tomorrow night?' I suggested.

'Okay. What d'you want to do?'

'Don't know. Go for a drink or something. I'll phone you.'

I left. Trish lived on the seventeenth floor of the block of flats, but I didn't take the lift. Half the time, it was out of order. The other half, some drongo had had a shit in it during the night. The block, slummy as it was, wasn't particularly bad for Glasgow's Maryhill. Trish hated it, but she was stuck there. It was all she could get from the council, and she couldn't afford to rent private property. The salary she earned as a primary-school teacher barely kept her in her present place. Even so, she was still making a hell of a lot more than me.

It took me about five minutes to walk down the stairs. I could've done it quicker, but I liked to read the graffiti that was scrawled on all the landings. It seemed that everybody'd been there except Kilroy. Finally I reached the ground, turned into the foyer and vomited my guts up.

Lying on the concrete floor was what had been a dog. I suppose it still was a dog, only now it was a dead dog that had been decapitated, then – it seemed – turned inside out. I think I could've handled that; what brought up a half pint of watery vomit was the sight of the maggots. There must've been hundreds of them, so many that the stinking, bloody carcass actually seemed to be writhing. It was between me and the entrance to the foyer, and it was so liberally spread across the floor that it was impossible to avoid it.

Eyes closed, I squelched my way to the door, walking right into two of Glasgow's finest. They looked at me and I looked at them, each of us waiting for someone else to speak. Then one of them said, 'You're in a hurry.'

'Take a look in there, Officer.' I motioned towards the door I'd just come out of.

The one who'd spoken took me by the arm. 'Come on, then.'

I shook him off. 'No thanks. I've had a look.'

He glared at me in approved Gestapo fashion. 'Don't be fucking cheeky.'

They were obviously used to playing Pinky and Perky, for at that point his partner said, 'Leave the boy alone. Look in there.'

'Right. Watch him, then,' said Pinky, pushing me aside. He went into the foyer. A pause. 'Fuck's sake.'

'Wait here, son,' Perky told me, and followed Pinky into the foyer. 'Fuck's sake.'

They both came back out, neither looking hungry. 'There's a dead dog in there,' Pinky told me.

'And some vomit,' added Perky.

I nodded.

'Did you do it?' asked Pinky.

'The vomit's mine. The corpse isn't,' I said.

'Somebody phoned and reported it. Was that you?'

I shook my head. 'I only found it a couple of minutes ago.'

'What d'you think happened?' Perky asked Pinky.

Pinky said nothing.

'Maybe it was suicide,' I suggested. 'Living in this place could even drive a dog to it.' The morning air was easing my nausea and I felt more like myself. 'Can I go?' I asked the Law.

'Can you fuck.' Pinky produced a notebook. 'We'll need some information first,' he said, face set in a Clint Eastwood scowl. 'Let's have your name for a start,' he said, as Perky began a conversation with his walkie-talkie.

'Gary Scott.'

'Address?'

'228 Laurel Gardens.'

'So, what're you doing here?' Pinky demanded, scribbling furiously in his notebook.

'I stayed the night with my girlfriend.' I was getting annoyed.

'Her name?'

'Patricia Donald.'

He noted it down. 'Have you ever been in trouble?'

'Yes. I've been sued for libel three times.'

He looked at me strangely. 'Libel?'

'Yes. Three times.' I smiled. I've always taken a perverted pride in my record for libel.

Hesitantly, Pinky said, 'What d'you do?'

'I'm editor of the *City Review*,' I told him.

'Fuck's sake!'

'Don't swear at the man!' said Perky, breaking away from his radio conversation.

'Sorry.' Pinky looked worried.

'It's okay,' I said, loving it.

'You see, we got this call, about a mutilated dog, then found you. Of course we had to be careful.'

'Of course you did. Don't worry about it.' I felt sorry for him; he was obviously worried he'd be the subject of an article attacking abuse of police power. 'But, look. About the dog. There might be a story there for me. D'you think it'd be okay for me to get someone to take a photo?' I asked.

Pinky looked uncertain. 'Mm-mm ... I don't –'

Perky interrupted him. 'It's fine by us, but I've just radioed for somebody to come and clean up. They'll be here in about ten minutes.'

'Shit.' That ruled out a photo by Raymond. I walked over to the car-park across the road and opened the boot of my car, a ninth-hand Citroen that'd cost three hundred quid and still started first time, sometimes. After a hurried search, I found the camera that Tricia had given me for my twenty-third birthday the year before. It'd never been used. I hoped it'd work okay.

8

# TWO

The offices of the *City Review* were in a dilapidated basement in the Gorbals. It was the best I could afford when I started the mag three years ago. All I had then was a bank loan and some talented friends who were willing to work for nothing, so I couldn't be fussy about premises. I promised myself I'd move upmarket if the mag became a success, but, now that I could move, I didn't want to.

And the *City Review* was a success – of sorts. At the start, I'd had to give it away free and depend on advertising for income. Soon, though, the magazine began to gather a small cult following, enough to allow me to start charging for it. For two years, the situation was the same: those who liked us loved us, those who didn't, hated us, and everyone else just ignored us.

Then, things started to change. We – or rather I, as editor – were sued twice for libel, and won, then a third time, and lost. The resulting publicity increased our sales by a third. Then I spent three months in prison for contempt of court, and our sales doubled. In the space of a year, the *City Review* had become one of Glasgow's top selling magazines. We were still loved by some and hated by others, but now nobody ignored us.

I expected that my financial lot would improve accordingly, but I was wrong. I took on seven full-time staff, which cost me plenty. Court cases leave quite a hole in your bank balance too. I was no longer living on the absolute breadline, but I wasn't far above it. But I felt sure that if I used profits to improve the mag rather than to pay myself an inflated wage, the financial benefits would be greater in the long term. In the meantime, I wasn't starving.

I arrived at the office at about ten. The mag was in the final week of production, meaning that everyone was having at least two nervous breakdowns at once. I didn't go into the main office, but went instead to the cubbyhole that served as my office. It was a tiny, cluttered room with a desk, a filing cabinet and a few tons of rubbish lying about.

I sat down at my desk and thought for a moment, then picked up the phone next to my old manual typewriter. I heard it ring next door in the main office, then Ian Stewart, the deputy editor, said, 'Hello?'

'Come on through, Ian.'

'Gary, when did you arrive?' He sounded harrassed.

'Just now. Come through.'

A moment later there was a quick rap on my door and Ian came in. He was — and still is, unless he's changed since yesterday — a cheerful, scruffy man in his mid-twenties. 'What's up?' he asked.

'Problem,' I said. 'How's production going?'

'Fine,' he said. 'Layout's nearly finished. We'll be ready for the printers tomorrow afternoon.'

I smiled at him.

'We won't, will we?' He sighed. 'What's up?'

'I'll explain later. I've got a news story that'll have to go into this issue. It can't wait till next month, so something'll have to go.'

He looked worried. 'Like what?'

'Mm ... Take out my feature on the slaughterhouses. That's evergreen, it'll keep till next month.'

He sighed again. 'Okay. It's going to delay us for a couple of days.'

'Can't help it. This is too good to miss out.'

'What is it?'

'I'll show you later. I'm just about to write the report.' I felt in my pocket and found the film I'd used to take photos earlier that morning. I handed it to Ian. 'Give this to Raymond. Tell him to develop it. The quality'll be shit, but it's all we've got. I'd to take them myself.' As Ian was leaving I added, 'Tell Raymond to prepare himself for a shock before he looks at it.'

Ian looked intrigued. 'I can't wait to see this.'

I opened my notebook as he left. I'd taken down four pages in shorthand from the interviews I'd done with Officers Pinky and Perky. I read through them, then put a sheet of A4 in my typewriter and got going.

An hour later, the report was finished. I went over it with a red pen and struck out a few unnecessary words and phrases, then did a word count. Five hundred. Nice and tight.

I went through to the main office. Hardly anyone seemed to notice I'd come in; they were all bent over layout boards. I tapped Ian on the shoulder and handed him the report. He looked at the title.

11

'*Maryhell?* Very good, Gary. That's one thing I've always admired about you – your total lack of sensationalism …'

I grinned. 'Read the article. This one merits sensationalism. Has Raymond done the photos yet?'

'He's doing them now.'

'Come through to my office,' I told Ian. 'How's about some coffee, Heather?' I asked the magazine secretary/dogsbody as we went out.

'I'll bring it through in a minute,' she answered.

In my office, Ian read my report. It consisted of a description of what I'd seen that morning, plus statements from Pinky and Perky that it'd happened before, though only to rats and cats.

Ian looked at me. 'The pigs say they think it was glue sniffers,' he remarked. 'Do you?'

'Not necessarily,' I said. 'It could've been glue sniffers, junkies or just some nutter. Whatever, it's a good opportunity to put the boot into Maryhill.'

'Whereabouts in Maryhill was this?' Ian asked.

'Trish's block of flats.'

'Christ. D'you think she might be in any danger?'

'Who knows? Anyone who could turn a dog inside out – and I'm not kidding, wait'll you see the photos – anyone who can manage that could probably do a human being a fair bit of harm.'

'Well, if we kick up enough shit, maybe the pigs'll find whoever did it,' Gary said.

I considered. 'Could we take out the editorial about Paul Campbell?'

Before Ian could answer, Heather came in with the coffee. 'There's a Rhona Jacobs coming to see you at noon,' she told me.

'Rhona? Oh, the new part-timer. Okay, send her in when she arrives.'

When Heather'd gone, Ian asked me, 'Why's the editorial to go?'

'Well, I think we should run one demanding something gets done about Maryhill,' I said. 'Would it be too much hassle to drop the Paul Campbell piece?'

'Not at all. Putting in the report'll delay us anyway.' He looked relieved, and I knew why. Ian hadn't been happy about the editorial in which I called Paul Campbell, a local MP who was thought to be cooking some charity's books, 'a liar, a cheat, a leech and a parasite.' Ian'd remarked once or twice that the piece would probably get me another stretch in Barlinnie.

'Right. Send the report to get typeset. Fuck off and leave me to write the editorial,' I told him.

'Okay. Are you to be disturbed?'

'Not before noon, unless it's to see the photos. Tell Raymond to bring them through as soon as they're ready.'

'Okay.' He went.

Alone, I started to write.

### EDITORIAL

In this issue, we describe the horrific mutilation of a dog, found in the foyer of a block of flats in Maryhill. This is not an isolated case. Police say that over the past few months the dead bodies of mice, rats and cats have been found in a similar condition in the same block.

This must stop, and the way to stop it is not to lock up the individuals responsible for this act. This behaviour is a symptom of the problem, not the problem itself. The problem is the stinking slum where this behaviour is taking place. Mary- hill is a cruel joke on Glasgow, a joke too sick to be funny. A sick environment produces sick people. 'Glasgow's Miles Better,' our Council boasts ...

*It is time they made it better for the people of Maryhill.*

It wasn't the greatest piece I'd ever written, in fact it was pretty poor. But it was okay for such a rush job. When I'd finished it, I showed it to Ian, who liked it, and we sent it to the typesetters.

We were sitting in my office when Heather phoned through. 'Rhona Jacobs is here.'

'Send her through,' I said.

Rhona was a small, slight girl of about twenty-one, with very dark hair and very pale skin. Her dark eyes were large and haunted. She came into my office wearing jeans and a jumper, and looked nervously from Ian to me. I'd never met her before; it was Ian who'd interviewed her for the job of part-time writer. She was to cover concerts in the city, and do some of the book reviews.

'Hello.' She looked uneasy. 'I'm Rhona Jacobs. You said to come at twelve ...'

I got up from my chair and held out my hand. 'Hi. I'm Gary Scott, the editor. Welcome aboard.'

She shook my hand. Her touch was firm, a little sweaty. She smiled. 'Thanks. I'm sure I'm going to enjoy working here.'

I grinned at her. 'Famous last words.' I motioned towards Ian. 'You've met Ian, the deputy editor?'

'Oh, yes.' She nodded. Ian smiled at her.

'Well,' I said, 'we're just about to go to press, so there's nothing very much for you to do. It'll be next week sometime before I know what I want you to do for the next issue, so you can spend the time settling in.'

'That's great. Thanks.'

There was a knock on my door. 'Come in.' Raymond, the magazine photographer, walked in with about half a dozen colour photos under his arm. 'Ah, you've done it. How'd they turn out?' I asked.

Raymond sat on the edge of my desk. He was a twenty-year-old trendoid who looked as though he'd been pulled out of the audience on *Top Of The Pops*. 'Jesus,' was all he said. 'Jesus, Gary.'

'Let's see them.' I took the photos from him, adding some introductions as an afterthought. 'Rhona, Raymond. Raymond, Rhona. Raymond works here sometimes ...' Raymond insulted me in return, but I didn't pick up what he said.

The photos were great. I'd expected some blurred snapshots, considering that they'd been taken by a poor photographer using a poor camera. But they were great. They didn't come close to the horror of the real

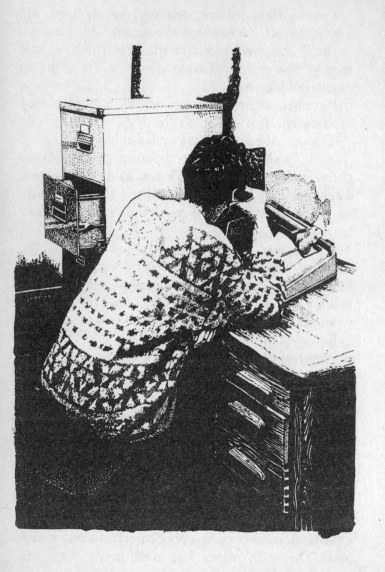

thing, but they were still wonderfully disgusting.

'Mm. Love-ly.' I handed them to Ian. 'What d'you think? Front page stuff, I reckon.'

'Fuck!' Ian looked shocked.

'You should've seen the real thing,' I told him.

'Can I have a look?' asked Rhona.

'You'll be sorry you asked,' said Ian, giving her the photos.

He was wrong. She just looked at them, then curiously at me. 'What's it about?' she asked.

'I was kind of wondering about that myself,' said Raymond.

'I stayed the night in a block of flats in Maryhill. When I left this morning, that's what I found in the foyer.'

'What is it?' asked Raymond.

'A dog.'

'What happened to it?'

'I wish I knew,' I said.

'That's odd.' Rhona was still studying the photos.

'I suppose it is,' I admitted. 'Words stronger than "odd" spring to mind, though.'

She shook her head. 'Not that.' She looked very closely at one of the pictures. 'Are those maggots on the ...'

'Yes. It was alive with them. It actually seemed to be moving.'

'That's what's odd.'

'How come?'

'Did you go through the foyer last night?' she asked me.

'Uh-huh.'

'And it wasn't there then?'

'No, I reckon I'd've noticed.'

'There shouldn't be maggots, then,' she said firmly.

My phone rang. I picked it up. 'Scott.'

It was Heather. 'Gary, is Ian with you? Andy and Glenn are fighting over the layout.'

'Shit. Okay, I'll send Ian through.' I put the phone down. 'Ian, the children aren't getting along in class. Can you go and see to them?'

'Yeah. Silly bastards.' He got up and went.

'I'd better go as well,' said Raymond. 'I've got more stuff to print up.'

When he'd gone, I looked at Rhona. 'Why shouldn't there be maggots?'

Patiently, she explained. 'Obviously, the dog must-'ve copped it during the night. In the space of a few hours, flies – lots of them – would've had to lay eggs on it. The eggs would hatch, and you'd have maggots. But that takes days, not hours. And would there be that many flies about on a cold summer night?'

'How could it've happened, then?'

'I don't know. That's why it's odd.'

I considered. 'If you're right, it's not odd. It's impossible.'

'But it happened, didn't it?'

'Oh, it happened.' I looked at the clock on my wall. It was almost one. 'Listen, d'you fancy coming for some lunch?'

'Where to?' she asked.

'There's a pizza place just around the corner,' I told her.

She smiled, and I liked it. 'Okay.'

I picked up my phone and spoke to Ian in the main office. 'I'm going for lunch,' I said. 'If anybody calls, say I'll be back about two.'

'All right,' he said. 'Are you going with Rhona?'

'How'd you know?' I asked, surprised.

'How'd you think?' He laughed, but it was a funny sort of laugh. 'If Trish calls, what'll I tell her?'

'Fuck off,' I said and hung up.

Rhona looked at me. 'What was that about?'

'Doesn't matter,' I said. 'Let's go.'

The café round the corner from our office was locally known as Salmonella Sam's, but it was handy and the food didn't actually kill you. I ordered a cheese and mushroom pizza. Rhona studied the menu for a minute. 'What d'you recommend?' she asked.

'You'd find my diet a bit limited, I said. 'I'm vegetarian. But I've heard the gammon steaks are nice.'

'That's out.' She smiled. 'I'm Jewish.'

'You sound like you're apologising,' I said. 'What's up?'

She shrugged. 'I'm not apologising. It's just that you never know how people are going to take it.' She hesitated. 'Being Jewish got me a broken jaw a couple of years ago.'

I grinned. 'Don't worry. I'd need more reason than that.' She laughed, and decided to order a seafood pizza.

'So, you're a practicing Jew?' I asked, wondering if they did it with gentiles.

'Not really. I used to practice a lot, but I'm good at it now.'

19

As we waited for the food to arrive, I said, 'I'll tell you, I'm very impressed.'

'By what?'

'You. Catching on about the maggots. I should've thought of it, and didn't. Neither did Ian, and he's an intelligent guy. But you picked up on it right away. I'm impressed.' I was so impressed I was starting to fancy her absolutely rotten . . . if I hadn't when I first saw her.

'So, how do you explain it?' she asked, ignoring the compliment.

'I can't,' I admitted.

'Couldn't the dog have been killed somewhere else, a couple of days ago maybe, and brought along this morning?'

'That occured to me, but no. It was definitely killed pretty recently. There was blood everywhere.' I paused. 'The closest I can get to an explanation is that maybe whoever killed the dog brought along some maggots and put them on the carcass.'

'But what for?' Rhona asked.

'What would anyone kill the dog like that for? We're probably not dealing with the most normal of people here, you know. I mean, you saw the photo; the dog was turned *inside out*.' I saw the waitress approaching with our food. 'Listen, d'you really want to talk about this over lunch?'

'Not really,' she said, but I got the impression it wouldn't bother her. 'So,' she said lightly, through her first mouthful of pizza, 'what's prison like?'

I laughed. 'If you only knew how many times I've

been asked that! Well, it wasn't too bad. It doubled sales of the mag.'

'I heard all about it when it happened,' she said. 'That was how I started reading the *City Review*. I'd heard of it before, but never read it. Then I read about you in the papers, and started buying the mag.' She looked at me sympathetically. 'I think it must've been horrible.'

'Mm. In all honesty, it's not an experience I'd care to repeat.'

'Why'd you do it? Why didn't you just give the name of your informant?'

I laughed. 'The papers made me out to be really heroic, but the truth is I didn't think they'd jail me. You see, I didn't knowingly violate the Official Secrets Act by publishing the article. My source was the one who'd signed under the Act, so he was the one who'd've copped the shit if I'd given away his identity. When the court ordered me to give his name, he came to see me and pleaded with me not to. So I didn't. I expected to be fined for contempt of court, but when they started talking about prison, I thought they were just trying to scare me. I couldn't believe it when the judge said three months!' I laughed again, re-membering.

'Would you have given them the guy's name if you'd known they'd put you in prison?'

'No,' I said.

'I didn't think so.'

'It wasn't pleasant, but it wasn't a nightmare either.

You can get through it okay as long as you're not flabby and self-indulgent. Once you accept that you're stuck there for three months it becomes quite interesting.'

Rhona said, through another mouthful of pizza, 'Once I started reading your articles in the *Review*, I was hooked. You're a very good writer.'

'You're only saying that because it's true,' I said modestly.

She finished her meal. 'Whereabouts do you live?' she asked.

'Laurel Gardens, over in the West End. How about you?'

'Cathcart.'

'Live with your folks?' I asked.

'Just my Mum. You?'

'Just me,' I told her. 'I had parents once, but I forget what I did with them.'

We stayed and talked for another half hour before leaving. As we walked back to the magazine office, I asked, 'Could I see you again ... maybe?'

'You'll see me for the rest of today, and tomorrow morning.'

'I know but I mean –'

She grinned at me. 'I know what you mean. All right.'

# THREE

That evening, I was sitting on my bed playing my guitar when the phone rang. I picked it up. 'Hello. Scott.'

'Gary, it's Trish.' She didn't sound in the best of moods.

'Oh, hi. How's things?'

'I've been trying to phone you all afternoon.'

'I was busy. You wouldn't believe what I found in your foyer this morning.'

'I know what you found. People've been talking about nothing else all day.'

'You sound nervous,' I said, with my usual insight and sensitivity.

'Of *course* I'm fucking nervous! There's obviously some kind of nutter prowling around here! If he'd do that to a dog, why wouldn't he do it to me?'

Why, indeed? 'Want me to come over?' I asked.

'No. I couldn't put up with you tonight,' she said.

'Thanks.' A pause. 'How'd you find out about the dog?'

'I told you, it's been the talk of the block. The girl who lives upstairs told me when I got home at lunchtime. She said a dog'd been found cut open, and that you were there.'

*Cut open?* I decided I'd better not say what it was really like. 'How'd she know I was there?' I asked.

'I don't know.'

'Mm. The police've obviously been telling stories.'

'Will I see you tomorrow night?' Trish asked.

'Sorry. I've got something arranged.' I felt a sudden pang of guilt. 'Listen, if you're really worried about what happened up there, d'you want to swap flats for a week or two?' I suggested.

'No, thanks. Living in your flat'd be like living with you,' she said flatly. 'I'll call you. Bye.' She hung up.

I went back to my guitar. I wasn't hurt by Trish's attitude towards me. I was too used to it. For more than a year I'd known well enough that she was indifferent to me as a person, and disliked my company most of the time. However, she liked being seen out with me because of my local notoriety. When I got out of the slam, one of the tabloids ran a front page photo of me embracing her, with the headline JAILED JOURNALIST UNITED WITH LOVER, and she revelled in it. But – I think – her main reason for keeping me around was quite simply that we were absolutely, indescribably great in bed.

Why'd I stick with her? For rather different reasons. I liked her, enjoyed her company. I liked the quickness of her wit, her erudition, her independence and grim refusal to feel sorry for herself. In short, I cared for her. I liked the fucking, too.

Next day, my news story and Editorial came back from the typesetters with – miraculously – no errors, so we were able to lay them out right away. Or, rather, Ian did.

I was on the phone to our printers at ten in the morning, arranging for them to come and pick up the stuff late that afternoon, when Ian came into my office. He was carrying a layout sheet and looked worried.

'What's up?' I asked when I'd finished my phone call.

'It's your story. It's too long.' He put the sheet on my desk.

I looked through my article. 'It's tight,' I said. 'There's nothing I can take out.' He nodded. I looked at the article on the same page. 'I'll just have to cut some of Glenn's stuff.'

'That'll be easy enough,' said Ian. 'He's overwritten it as usual. He won't like it being chopped, though.'

'He can dislike it, then. I don't give too much of a shit.' I've always done well staff-wise; by luck rather than good judgement on my part, everyone who's worked for the mag has either been good, or wanted to become good. Glenn Lenzie, features editor, was the exception. An arrogant, condescending little snob, he'd managed to convince Ian and me that he could write. We'd taken him on, and had regretted it ever since. His articles were more than just long-winded; they were purple. He did not understand even the basic principles of journalism, and he would not be taught. He made no secret of the fact that he considered himself the world's greatest living writer, and despised all journalists as semi-literate hacks. What he lacked in talent and hair, he made up for in flab and body odour.

The fact that I disliked Lenzie so intensely usually

worked to his advantage. Conscious of this dislike, I was determined to be scrupulously fair to him, so I tended to take more shit from him than I would from others more talented. So, much as I hated his pretentious, boring articles-cum-adolescent prose poems, I allowed them to appear in the mag after the minimum of editing.

This time, though, something, somewhere, had to be cut. I read through Lenzie's article, a story of a CND rally. *'The sun looked like a fading Catherine wheel,'* I read aloud, *'as blankets of fog came down.* Fuck's sake!'

Ian made a face. 'Chronic, isn't it?'

'Well, at least there's plenty to cut,' I said. 'Can you tell Glenn to come through?'

I steeled myself to be pleasant to Lenzie as Ian went to get him. 'Hi, Glenn,' I said as he came in. Ian hadn't come back.

Lenzie glowered at me suspiciously. 'What's up?' he said. He was fat and smelly and looked twenty years older than the twenty-six he was. I told myself firmly that I was going to be nice.

'It's this article of yours, Glenn. I hate to say it, but we're going to have to cut some of it. I've got to put a news story in, and it can't be cut.' Lenzie looked at me and said nothing. 'Since it's your article, I'll let you decide what's to go,' I said. 'But it'll have to be a few paragraphs.'

'There's nothing to be cut,' he said sullenly. 'It's all relevant. I can't cut it.'

'Okay. I'll try, and you see what you think,' I said. I then went over the piece with my red pen, cutting out all repetition and needlessly lyrical passages. 'There. What d'you think?' I asked Lenzie.

He looked it over. 'No. You've destroyed the article,' he bleated. 'You've turned it into a piece of journalism.'

*Be nice, Gary!* I told myself again. 'That's what it's meant to be, Glenn,' I said patiently. 'You see, this is a magazine. I want pieces of journalism because I'm a journalist. And guess what?' I said gently, as he started to protest. 'You're a journalist too. That's what you're employed as. Now, we've got two pieces of *journalism* here. Both have to go in the mag. There's not enough space. One can be cut and the other can't. So which one should be cut?' *Well done, Gary.*

Lenzie shook his balding head haughtily. 'No. No! I'm holding out.'

At that, my temper just gave way. There was something in his tone, his infuriating, self-important manner, that made reasonable argument out of the question.

I didn't blow up, though. I slipped into a quiet rage. 'Tell me something, Glenn,' I said in a low voice. 'What do you mean by that? What do you mean you're *holding out?*'

He looked uncomfortable. 'Well —'

'Because I'd really like to know, Glenn. I'd like to know how you're going to *hold out.* You see — maybe you haven't realised — I'm editor of this magazine. You know, that's why people address letters to me "Editor". So tell me, Glenn, how're you going to hold out? Tell me, please. *Because I really want to know, Glenn!*' He looked as though he might cry. In a calmer voice I said, 'If you can't tell me, take the sheet, go next door and lay it out with Ian. I'll come through and give you a hand in about ten minutes. And don't ever try to push me around again.' Without a word, he took the layout sheet and went.

I gave myself ten minutes to cool off, then went through to the main office. Everyone was busy sticking bits of copy down on layout sheets. Andy, our graphic artist, was showing Rhona how it was done. I went over to them and examined their sheet. As always, Andy's work was perfect.

'Are we still okay for tonight?' I whispered to Rhona. She smiled and nodded.

I helped Ian and Lenzie lay out the page we'd been fighting over. The latter pulled the odd face or two as we cut out large chunks of nothing in particular from his article, but he didn't say anything. With all of us working on the layout, the mag was ready for the printers when they arrived at four-thirty that afternoon. They promised it'd be on the streets the following morning.

I'd had no lunch, so I went round to Salmonella Sam's for a carry-out pizza, then returned to the office. Everybody had gone home except for Ian, Raymond and Rhona. 'Hi,' I called as I came into the main office, pizza in hand. 'Any calls for me?'

Ian said nothing. Raymond got up and headed for the toilet, and Ian followed him. Rhona said, 'Yes. Your girlfriend phoned about five minutes ago.'

I put my pizza down on a desk, frantically trying to

28

think of some explanation. Rhona just looked at me. 'She's just a girlfriend of sorts,' I said weakly.

'Well, we're even, then. I've got a boyfriend. Of sorts.' She smiled coldly.

'What about tonight?' I said.

'What about tonight?'

'Is it off?' I asked.

'Not unless you want to call it off.'

'I don't.'

'Then it's not.' She put on her coat. 'I'm off now. See you later, okay?'

'Fine,' I said as she left.

Slowly, I sat on a desk and began to eat my pizza. After a couple of minutes Ian and Raymond returned. 'Coast clear?' asked Ian. I nodded glumly. 'Sorry,' he said. 'She was first to the phone when it rang.'

'My own fault. I should've thought that Trish might ring,' I said.

Raymond picked up his camera case and bag. 'When'll you need me next, Gary?' he asked. I'd promised him some time off once this issue went to press. He'd earned it. You could ask him to work overtime at a moment's notice and he'd never complain.

'You can have a week off at least,' I said. 'Phone me a week today and I'll let you know when to come back.'

'Thanks,' he said. 'If you happen to need me before then, give me a ring. It'll be cool.'

As Raymond left, I called after him, 'You did really great this issue.' He laughed and waved as he went out the door.

I looked at Ian. 'If you want to hold on till I finish my pizza, I'll give you a lift home.'

'Okay.' There was silence for a moment, then he said, 'I'm surprised at you.'

'About what?' I asked, knowing full well, but hoping he'd let it go.

He didn't. 'I know it's none of my business. But in a way it is. If you want to two-time Trish, that's your affair. But you're supposed to be ... well, a *professional*. How ethical is it to employ someone, and ask her out almost as soon as she's through the door?'

'Do you fancy her yourself?' I asked.

'No, I don't!' he retorted, and I knew he wouldn't lie.

'Okay, then. First, regarding Trish. You don't know what you're talking about, so keep your nose out. Regarding Rhona —' I smiled 'I'm totally out of order. You're absolutely right. You know how I've always felt about fucking the staff. I'm behaving totally unethically.'

'Why're you doing it?' he asked.

I had no answer.

'You really like her?'

'Uh-huh. But that's no excuse.'

'No,' he agreed. 'It's not.'

'I know. I'm acting like shit. I'm not happy about it either. Come on, let's go.'

We locked up, then went out to my car. I got it to start at the third attempt, which wasn't too bad. I headed for the Merchant City, where Ian lived. 'What'd you think of this issue?' I asked, by way of making conversation.

'I think you're pushing your luck with the cover,' he said. Ian had been reluctant to put the picture of the mutilated dog on the front page, saying it was too horrible and would put potential buyers of the mag off. When I said I wanted to run the photo in full colour, he told me I'd taken leave of my senses. Knowing he was talking sense, but believing the photo deserved the front page spot, I'd compromised by running it in black and white.

'D'you think we'll get shit for it?' I asked as I drove.

'We might,' he said. 'We'll definitely get a few letters of complaint at least. It's a disgusting photo.' Suddenly, he grinned. 'That apart, I think this month's is the best issue ever.'

I was relieved to hear that. Ian had been with me since I set up the mag. In those three years, we'd had dozens of editorial disagreements, with him threatening to resign on one occasion, and me almost angry enough to fire him on another. But, even during our most heated disputes, I still had a tremendous respect for his opinion, valuing it above that of any other. He'd taken care of the mag while I was in prison, putting his own head on the chopping block by calling the judge who sentenced me 'this corrupt Government's arse-licking servant', and the trial 'an evil kangaroo court that imprisoned a journalist for upholding the integrity of his profession'. When I read that, I half expected Ian to join me as a guest of Her Majesty.

In short, he was a guy I had a lot of time for.

As I let him out of the car I said. 'Don't worry about

things Rhona-wise. It'll work out.'

'Hope so. See you tomorrow.' I sat in the car and watched him go into his close. I hoped so, too.

When I got home, I rang Trish. 'Hi, it's Gary. You rang me at work?'

'Uh-huh.' She sounded quite cheery. 'Just to find out if you fancy coming over here tomorrow night.'

What could I tell her? Nothing yet. 'All right. What time?'

'About seven?'

'Fine. How're you feeling?' I asked. 'Still nervous?'

'Not so bad now. It's passed. Bye.' With her usual abruptness, she hung up.

I put the phone down and sat looking at it. 'So,' I said aloud, mimicking Trish's voice, 'did you get the mag to press on time? Yes, Trish.' This last in my own voice. 'Is it a good issue, Gary? Yes, Trish, it's a very good issue, *and I appreciate your fucking interest.*'

I'd arranged to meet Rhona outside the Glasgow Film Theatre at eight. I got there at a quarter to. I was feeling pretty good. I'd had a shower and shave, and saturated myself with aftershave. I was wearing the suit I usually reserved for TV appearances and funerals.

Rhona arrived about a minute late, wearing her usual jumper, jeans and training shoes. 'Hi.' She smiled. 'Been waiting long?'

I smiled back. 'Hours.'

'Liar.' We went into the cinema. I tried to pay for us both, but she insisted on going Dutch. She didn't like the film much, though I did. About a third of the way through the film, I put an arm around her. There was no response. She didn't draw away, but didn't cuddle against me either.

Afterwards, we drove over to the West End and went to Basil's, a vegetarian restaurant near my flat. It was a friendly, pleasantly Spartan place that served excellent food. As Rhona and I ate succulent nut roasts, I made a mental note to give the place a favourable mention in the next issue of the mag.

'Tell me about your girlfriend,' Rhona said suddenly, as she ate.

'What about your boyfriend?' I answered defensively.

'I asked first,' she said.

'All right. I know I should've mentioned her before I asked you out.'

'Uh-huh. You should.'

'Sorry. Well, her name's Trish. I've known her for about two years.' I stopped, unable to decide how to go on.

'Are you in love with her?' asked Rhona.

'No. I used to be. Or I thought so at the time. But not now.' I hesitated, then decided to be blunt. 'Actually, she doesn't like me very much. We're not so much boyfriend and girlfriend as sleeping partners. I'd probably have finished it ages ago if it wasn't for the fact that I like to have sex on tap as much as anyone, and I've never met anybody else to leave her for.'

'So why did you ask me out?'

While I was trying to think of an answer, I found myself telling the truth. 'Because I've never felt so at ease in anybody's company before.'

Rhona ate in silence for a moment. 'I used to live with a guy called Peter. I still see him. He's still my boyfriend, sort of.'

'Why'd you stop living with him?'

'He hit me. He still does, sometimes. I moved back to my Mum's after I tried to kill myself.' I looked at her sharply to see if she was joking, then saw she wasn't.

'How'd you do it?' I asked, trying to keep the anger out of my voice. She rolled back the sleeve of her jumper to show me her left wrist. The scar was still quite clear. 'Can't have been that long ago,' I said.

'Couple of months.'

'Why'd you still take it?'

'I love him. I think.'

We finished our food and had some wine. 'So, what's going to happen?' I finally asked her.

'Don't know. Let's wait and see.'

'Mm, that's a nice cliché. Haven't heard it for ages,' I said. She laughed and stuck her tongue out at me.

It was about eleven. I asked her, 'D'you want to come back to my flat for coffee or something?'

She grinned at me. 'I'll skip the something, but the coffee's a good idea.'

The waitress brought our bill. I wanted to pay it, but Rhona opened her purse and counted out six pounds, the bill being twelve. 'I pay my share.'

'On the wages I'm paying you, you can't afford to,' I told her. 'I'll get it.'

'If you don't let me pay half, I'm not going out with you again.' She was smiling when she said it, but I think she meant it.

'Okay.' I gave in, we paid the bill, then left and drove the short distance to my flat.

As I stopped the car outside my close, Rhona asked, 'Does your girlfriend live in that block of flats where you found the dog? Is that why you spent the night there?'

'Uh-huh.'

'Aren't you worried about her?'

'A bit,' I admitted. 'But don't talk about Trish now.' I leaned over and kissed her lightly on the cheek. She didn't slap my face. I moved my mouth over to hers and kissed her very gently, taking her in my arms as I did. I pulled her against me, kissing her harder. Her tongue caressed mine. Her hands were on the back of my head and neck, and her small, bony body rubbed against me. She groaned softly. I bent and started kissing her neck, as I felt her tiny breasts through her jumper.

Then I let her go. 'This is a bit public,' I said in a voice not my own. 'Let's go up to the flat.'

Rhona sat back in her seat, took a deep breath. Her face was scarlet, her hair tousled. Her dark eyes looked enormous. 'No,' she said in a tone of voice very similar to mine. 'I think I'd better just go home.'

'Why?'

'It's going a bit too fast for my liking. And I *like* it too much for my liking.' She smiled shakily.

'What's the problem, then?'

'I don't really know. But I'm going home.'

'Okay.' I sighed. 'I'll drive you.'

'No, that's okay.'

'It's no problem,' I said.

'I know. But I want to be on my own. I want to have a think, so I'll take a taxi.'

'Are you sure?'

'Yes.' She opened the car door on her side. 'I'm not supposed to be working tomorrow, but I'll either come in or phone you, okay?'

I nodded.

She got out of the car, then leaned in and kissed me quickly. 'Thanks, Gary. You're a really nice person.'

I sat in the car and watched her until she was out of sight, then went upstairs to my flat. I felt hot, and painfully frustrated. I was a walking horn.

I sat in my living room drinking tea for around half an hour. I felt a little less horny, but not much. I didn't feel like sleeping, but too tired to read or play my guitar.

I was in the bathroom brushing my teeth when the doorbell rang. I rinsed out my mouth and went to answer it, knowing for some reason it would be Rhona.

'Hi.' She stood dripping all over my doormat, smiling ruefully. 'I'm wet.'

'So I see.' I stepped away from the door. 'Come in.' She followed me into the hall. I took her wet jacket and shoes from her. 'What brought you back?' I asked.

'I got a taxi to the station, then wished I'd stayed here,' she said simply. 'So I walked back. I couldn't get another taxi, and it *poured*.'

'I believe you.' Her jeans were stuck to her legs. 'Go through to my bedroom. You'll find a dressing-gown hanging on the door. I'll make you some coffee.'

'Okay.' She ran a hand through her wet hair. 'Can I have a towel?'

'In the bathroom.' I pointed to the door. 'Help yourself.'

I went to the kitchen and made coffee for her and tea for myself, then took it through to the living room and set it on the coffee table. Rhona came in a few minutes later, wrapped in my towelling dressing-gown, which was much too big for her. The sleeves flapped past her hands, the gown trailed on the carpet behind her and she looked like a child. She sat down on the sofa next to me. 'I hung my clothes on the pulley in your bathroom, okay?'

'Fine,' I said.

She sipped her coffee and looked around the room. 'This really is a lovely flat. D'you own it?'

'Yes. I bought it about a year ago, just before I went into the slam.'

Rhona looked at the alcove where the desk and typewriter were. There was a sheet of A4 in the machine, and a ring binder next to it. 'Are you writing a book or something?'

'No, a play. A TV script, if I ever get it finished. The BBC read a synopsis and said they were interested, but that was eight months ago. They've probably forgotten. I keep meaning to finish it, but I've been too busy. And too lazy.'

There was a brief silence, then Rhona said, 'Aren't you going to kiss me again?'

'Do you want me to?' I said warily.

'Well, I didn't walk back here in the rain for a cup of

coffee. I've got plenty of that at home.'

'Are you sure?'

'Uh-huh. Two whole jars of it.'

'I mean about – Well, look what happened earlier.'

'I was just surprised at myself. I'm okay now.'

'Oh.'

'Are you going to kiss me or what?' she said, grinning.

I put my teacup down. 'Come here.'

She came to me quickly, fiercely. She pushed me back on the sofa, kissing me hard, hands finding my belt and fumbling with it. 'Your specs are steaming up,' she said breathlessly. I took them off. Rhona lay on top of me, and I felt her small pointed tongue in my mouth, her teeth nibbling my lips. I slipped my dressing-gown off her and kissed and sucked at her breasts. She undid my fly and put her hand on my cock. I gasped and shuddered.

Rhona looked worried. 'Did I hurt you?'

'No.' I laughed hoarsely. 'This sofa's okay for a midget like you, but I'm getting squashed. Let's go to bed.'

We were lucky to make it to the bedroom; I stopped to kiss her in the hall, and we nearly ended up fucking there and then, on the floor. Then we were in bed, and I was inside her, and her dark eyes were like saucers in the lamplight, and she was screaming and writhing, and our orgasms lasted so long it was like we were coming in slow motion.

Afterwards we lay and held each other and just kissed for a long time before either of us spoke. Then she said, 'Can I use your phone? I'd better let my Mum know I won't be home tonight.'

'Of course,' I said, stroking her hair. 'But won't she be in bed? It's after one.'

'I doubt it,' said Rhona, but she was wrong. There was no answer when she called home. As she came back to bed, I reflected that she was very ordinary looking, even plain, yet she gave the impression of a strange, haunted beauty. Where it came from I still don't know.

'Maybe it's as well she's asleep,' I said, as I switched off the lamp. 'What would she have said when you told her you were staying the night here?'

She kissed me in the darkness. 'I was going to say I was spending the night with a friend, so her first question'd be "Is it a boy?" Her second'd be "Is he Jewish?" '

'What would you have said?'

'No and yes.' She giggled. 'A great virtue, honesty.'

I laughed. 'Goodnight.'

'It has been so far.'

# FOUR

I was wakened at seven in the morning by the ringing of the phone. It woke Rhona too. 'Ignore it,' she mumbled, cuddling against me.

'Can't. It might be Ian. There might be a problem.' I got out of bed, went through to the living room and answered the phone. 'Scott.'

'Hi, it's me.' It was Trish, but she sounded strange.

'What's up? Are you okay?' I was concerned.

'Gary, remember what happened to that dog?'

'Has it happened again?'

'Sort of,' she said. 'This time it's happened to a seven-year-old girl.'

'Fuck's sake.' I sat down. My bowels were threatening to move. 'When was this?'

'They just found her. Or rather, Lesley next door did. She went missing late last night. I thought you might like to know, so I called you, but –'

'I was out. Sorry.'

'But Lesley was going down to the shops this morning, and she found the body on the back stairs.' A pause. 'What was left of the body, I mean. Lesley's in shock.'

'I can imagine,' I said. 'I saw the dog.'

'Gary, bits of the kid were stuck to the *ceiling*.'

'Jesus!' I honestly thought I might puke. Then I said, 'So Lesley called the police?'

'No. She came screaming to my door, and I called them. She's in my bed now.'

'Trish, d'you think she'd speak to me later? Give me an interview?'

'I don't know. I'll ask her later.' Trish laughed harshly. 'Callous bastard.'

'If I don't speak to her, the dailies will, anyway. How about the kid's parents? D'you know their names?'

'No. They live down on the third floor. I just know them to nod to. I can find out their names, though. Phone me at work this afternoon.'

'I will. Thanks,' I said. 'How're you taking all this? Are you okay?'

'So far. I don't think I've taken it in yet. Anyway, I'd better go.'

'Okay, I'll call you later. Take it easy.'

'Bye.' She rang off.

I went back to the bedroom. Rhona was sitting up in bed, drinking a glass of water. She looked gorgeous, but Venus couldn't've given me the horn at that moment. 'What's up?' asked Rhona.

My clothes lay in a heap on the floor. I picked up my underpants and put them on. 'A seven-year-old girl's been found up in Maryhill. Killed the same as the dog.' I put my trousers on.

'Christ! Where?'

'The same block of flats.' I took the trousers off again, went to a drawer, got a pair of jeans and put them on instead.

'Where your girlfriend lives?' The word 'girlfriend' sounded incongruous coming from a girl lying naked in my bed.

'Yes. That was her on the phone.'

'What're you going to do?'

Before I could answer, the phone rang again. This time, it was Ian. 'Hi, Gary? Trouble. I warned you about that photo on the front page, didn't I?'

'What's the problem?'

'I've just had Tam Fisher on the blower.' Fisher was the manager of John Menzies department store, and he didn't like me. 'He says John Menzies aren't going to sell this issue with a photo like that. They're going to send all their copies back.'

'Fuck!' John Menzies was one of our main retailers, and we were one of their biggest-selling magazines locally. I knew they wouldn't approve of the front page, but I didn't think they'd refuse to sell it. 'I'll speak to Fisher,' I said.

'That'll make his day,' Ian said caustically. 'I tried to talk him round, but he says the decision isn't his.'

'Bollocks. Whose decision is it, then?' I demanded. Ian didn't answer. He knew as well as I did that Fisher was just afraid of getting his knuckles rapped if there were any controversy over the mag.

I briefly told Ian about the dead kid, to which he reacted as you'd expect. 'I'll talk to you later,' I said, and hung up.

In the bedroom, I finished dressing. 'I'm going to have to leave right now,' I told Rhona, who was still in bed. 'But you can lie on if you like. I'll leave you a spare key.'

43

'No. I'm coming with you.' She got out of bed. 'This is getting interesting.'

At ten that morning, I was sitting in my office, flicking through a copy of the magazine. Ian was right, I thought. It *was* the best issue ever. And I still reckoned I was right to run the photo.

Tam Fisher, resident tin god at John Menzies, had taken a bit of convincing. I'd arrived there at nine, when they were just about to open, and asked to see him. I went through to his office when he didn't appear, and shit and fan became one. Paragons of logical debate, we screamed at each other for five minutes until Rhona followed me into the office and calmed things down.

'I can't *possibly* put it on the shelves,' he insisted. 'It's your own fault. You should've known not to wun a photo like that on the fwont page. It's a *disgwace*. You don't appweciate the twouble I could find myself in if I stock this issue.'

'Look.' I was trying not to lose my temper again. 'The photo was necessary.'

'*Necessawy*? Necessawy for what? To disgust our customers? To put them off buying your wag?'

I nearly blew up again, but didn't. 'The photo's justified by the story. It's important that people notice it.'

Rhona said, 'A little girl's just been murdered in the same spot.'

Fisher's eyes popped. 'Weally?'

'Weally,' I agreed. 'It's important to draw people's

attention to what goes on in that place. And, whatever shit it might stir, the photo won't put people off buying the magazine. If anything, it'll boost sales. Our regular readers won't be put off, and the photo'll attract sickos who wouldn't normally buy the mag.'

Fisher was silent for a moment, his dislike for me wrestling with his business sense. The latter won. 'All wight. I'll wisk it.'

'Thanks.' I forced myself to be pleasant. 'I appreciate it.'

And so it did come to pass that John Menzies did stock the *City Review*, and the public did come forth unto John Menzies and other stores and did buy the *City Review* in great numbers, and, verily, the retailers did sing and give thanks unto me for the shocking photo.

So, like I said, ten o'clock found me at my desk, crowing over the brilliance of the mag. We'd already had a few phone calls, some from other publications to praise the content of this issue, a few from stiff-arsed numbskulls who never bought the mag anyway, complaining about the front page. 'I'm sorry,' I told one of them politely. 'I think you must be confusing me with somebody who gives a shit.' And put the phone down. It's nice to be nice.

At ten-fifteen, I phoned Maryhill Police Station. The pigs had no comment to make about the death of the child, save that her name was Clare Gibney and the police were treating her death as murder. I asked to speak to Pinky and Perky, but was told that Constables Young and Jamieson wouldn't be in the station until that afternoon. I said I'd call back.

Rhona was in the main office. I rang through and Heather, the mag secretary, answered. 'Can you tell Rhona to come through?'

'Of course,' replied Heather, ever helpful. 'D'you want a cup of tea? I've just put some on.'

'Yeah, please.' I put the phone down.

Rhona came in without knocking, and sat on my desk. She was glowing: she'd thoroughly enjoyed the events of the morning so far. 'What's up?'

'Nothing,' I said. 'I've phoned the police, and they can't tell me anything. I'm going to speak to my police contacts later, but nothing's really likely to happen. You're not supposed to be working today, so you'd be as well going home.'

She looked disappointed. 'Are you sure? It was really interesting.'

'Certain,' I said, and laughed. 'I really like your interest, but there's nothing for you to do. And you'll give me a guilt complex if you hang around here when I'm not paying you to. Fuck off home and relax. Watch *Play School* or something.'

She grinned. 'Yes, my lord.' She bent over my chair and kissed me firmly on the mouth. 'I'll phone you.'

As Rhona left, Heather came in with my tea. 'Here you are.' She set it down on the desk in front of me.

'Thanks,' I said. Heather was plump, fair-haired and astonishingly clever. She was nineteen years old and did the work of two secretaries and one receptionist, but received one salary. 'What d'you think of the mag this month?' I asked her.

'I think it's great,' she said. She hesitated. 'Gary, I

47

don't like to tell tales, but –'

'What's the matter?'

'It's Glenn. Since he came in this morning, he's really been slagging you off.'

'What's he saying?'

'That you're a bully, and you don't know anything about writing. He's saying it in front of visitors too. And Ian's defending you, so it's getting pretty ugly.'

'Tell Glenn and Ian to come through here.' I sipped my tea.

Heather looked worried. 'You're not going to let on I told you, are you?'

'No. I'm not going to mention that I know. But Mr Lenzie's overdue a spanking.'

When Ian and Lenzie arrived, I could see from their expressions that they'd been arguing. Ian and I went into our SS interrogation routine, with Ian sitting on the edge of my desk and Lenzie standing uncomfortably before us.

'I've a couple of things I want to discuss with you, Glenn, and I'd like Ian to hear them, too.'

'What?' he said sullenly.

'In the past, I've been accepting pieces of overwritten, purple dog-shit from you, and publishing them as articles. Because I don't like you, Glenn.' He made to say something, but I cut in. 'Shut your hole, I'm not finished.' Ian, who hated confrontation, looked unhappy. 'I really don't like you, Glenn,' I went on. 'I think you're a pathetic, whining little turd. And because you're so pathetic, I've been nice to you. But you know, and I know, that you don't do your job. And

48

you're bad for magazine morale, as well as being incompetent.'

'What are you saying?' he demanded, running a greasy hand over what hair he still had.

'I'm saying you're no longer features editor, Glenn. You won't be writing any more features. From now on, you'll be doing basic news reports. And if you overwrite them I'll fire you.'

'I'm not a *reporter!*' Lenzie said the word in the same tone as I might say *child molester*. 'I won't have you turn me into a *hack!*'

'You think we're hacks, don't you?' Ian asked him. He didn't answer.

I made a decision, one I should've made long before. 'Get out of here, Glenn. You're fired,' I said. 'You can have a month's salary in lieu of notice.' He tried to speak, but I sprang from my seat, opened the door and pushed him out. 'Heather'll write you a cheque. Fuck off, and don't ever come into this office again.'

Lenzie gave me a look that was pure hatred. If nobody's ever looked at you that way, I can't describe it. 'You cunt,' he breathed. 'You stinking cunt. You'll be sorry you did this.'

I slammed the door in his face.

'Was I out of order?' I asked Ian, who looked upset. I knew he wouldn't be slow to criticise me if I was.

'No. You should've given him the boot ages ago.' He shook his head. 'But what a fucking morning! And it's not even eleven yet.'

I laughed. 'It can only get better.'

'Mm.' He didn't seem convinced. 'I take it from

Rhona's presence this morning that you fucked her last night?'

'Do you?' I asked evasively.

'All right.' He sighed. 'I won't press you. But watch what you're doing, Gary, okay?'

'I'm doing my best.'

'So,' he said, changing the subject, 'what about this dead kid?'

'I've phoned the pigs, and they're treating it as murder. That's all they'd say. I'm going to call them back later today, and see if I can speak to the pair I bumped into when I found the dog. And Trish said she might be able to arrange an interview with the girl who found the kid, and put us on to the kid's parents. But we'll have to go easy there. They won't be the happiest of people right now.'

At one that afternoon, I phoned the primary school where Trish taught, and asked to speak to her. 'Hi, Gary,' she said when she came on the line. 'I've asked Lesley if you can interview her. She says okay.'

'Great. When?' I asked.

'Today if you like. But go easy with her, she's still in quite a state. Here's her number.' She gave it to me and I scribbled in my notepad.

'What about the dead kid's parents?'

'Their names are Brian and Margaret Gibney. The girl was called Clare Gibney.'

I didn't tell her I knew that already. 'D'you know their phone number?' I asked.

'Yes. I got it out of the directory. But they probably won't be there. I'd expect them to be with relatives or

50

something.' I wrote down the number as she gave it to me.

'So how're you feeling?' I asked.

'Scared shitless, but I'll be okay,' she said. 'Will I still be seeing you tonight?'

'Yeah, of course,' I said. 'I don't know what time, though. I've got a lot to do. But I'll call you.'

'Okay,' she said. Then, surprisingly, she added, 'I read the magazine today. I think it's really terrific.'

'Thanks,' was all I could say. 'I'll have to go now. Lock your door when you get home, and don't open it till you know it's me.'

'All right. Don't worry. Bye.' She rang off.

I called Maryhill Police Station again, and asked to speak to Pinky or Perky. Perky came on. 'Constable Jamieson here.'

'Hi, it's Gary Scott. Remember me?'

'Of course, Mr Scott. I take it you're interested in the Clare Gibney murder?'

'Uh-huh. I hear it was just like the dog?'

'It wasn't me that found it, but yes. As far as I know it was the same as the dog.'

'Actually, I heard it was worse.'

'What d'you mean?' he said cautiously. 'Of course it was worse. It was a child this time.'

'I mean, I heard that bits of her were stuck to the ceiling.'

'Who told you that?' Perky said sharply.

'An informed source,' I answered blandly. 'Is it true?'

'Yes.' He took a deep breath. 'Mr Scott, I really shouldn't be telling you any of this.'

'Oh, come on! I'll find out anyhow,' I lied. 'Don't worry, I'm not going to print your name. Right now, I'm just trying to find out how much is known about what happened. Could I speak to the cops who found the corpse?'

'No, that's not possible,' he said firmly.

'Well, do you know what happened?' I asked.

'All I can say is that the child was severely mutilated, by a person or persons unknown, but who we're very keen to have a word with.'

'Fuck's sake! Where'd you learn that line? *The Sweeney*?' I got hold of my temper again. 'Look, people have a right to know about this. If the murderer's still around, people're in danger. It's just as much public business as police business.'

There was a long hesitation, then he said, 'Strictly between you and me, Mr Scott, we haven't a fucking clue what happened. All right?'

That terrified me more than if he'd said the killer was an indestructible being from outer space. 'Tell me just two things more,' I said gently. 'Were there maggots on the corpse?'

'So you've realised about that too. Yes, there were. And we can't figure it out either. What's your other question?'

'You're shit scared, aren't you?'

'Yes, Mr Scott, I am. We all are,' he answered simply. 'Is there anything else?'

'No, that's it. Thanks.'

When I'd hung up I just sat and looked at the phone

for a couple of minutes. First animals. Then a child. Then –

There was a knock on my door, and I nearly jumped out of my chair. 'Come in,' I called, in a quavering voice.

'Are you all right?' asked Ian, coming in. 'You sound like you've been kicked in the balls.'

I felt about five years old, and Ian and I both knew where I'd been at that age, where I was born. I felt small and scared and he was my best friend and I nearly cried and I nearly told him what I was so afraid of and then I couldn't.

'Ian, can you do me a favour?' I said in a whisper. 'Can you give me a hug?'

He grinned and started to make some joke about latent homosexuality, then realised I wasn't kidding. 'Come here.' I got out of my chair and he hugged me. I trembled violently in his arms. 'It's Maryhill, isn't it?' he said.

'Uh-huh.'

'Why're you so terrified of that place, Gary? What happened to you up there?'

'I don't really know,' I said truthfully. 'It's what's happening there now that scares me.'

# FIVE

I arrived at Warriston Court, Maryhill, at three-thirty. As I entered the foyer, I remembered the dog that'd been spread all over it. I felt like taking the lift instead of climbing the back stairs, but I forced myself to go up the seventeen flights of stairs to the flat where Lesley Tobin, Trish's neighbour, lived. Except for the two policemen standing at the door leading to the third floor corridor, there was nothing to suggest that a child had been found horribly murdered there that very morning.

I'd had to phone four times before Lesley finally answered with a hollow 'Hello?'

'Hi, Lesley? My name's Gary Scott. I'm editor of the –'

'Oh, Tricia's boyfriend. She said you'd phone.' She sounded slow, dopey. I guessed she'd taken some kind of sedative.

'That's right.' I tried to sound cheerful and reassuring. 'I thought you might like to talk to me about what happened today.' I paused, then added, 'If you feel up to it, that is. Trish said you got a bit of a shock.' Another astonishing display of sensitivity and understanding from Gary.

'I'm all right now.' She didn't sound it. 'I can speak to you today if you like.'

'That'd be great. Are you sure?'

'Yes. But bring some ID so's I know it's you.'

'I will. What time should I come over?' I asked.

'As soon as you like.'

I'd headed over there right away. Now I stood at her door, which was next to Trish's, and rang her bell. I heard her approach, then a female voice called, 'Who is it?'

'Gary Scott.'

'Did you bring ID?'

'Uh-huh.' I slipped my press card through the letterbox. A moment later, Lesley opened the door.

She was a spotty, anaemic-looking girl in her late twenties. She wore a dressing gown and her hair was tousled. She obviously wasn't long out of bed, and I decided that my guess that she was doped had been right. She gave me a sort of sick smile. 'Come in.' She handed me back my card.

I followed her through the hall to the living room and sat on the sofa. 'D'you want some tea?' she asked me.

'Only if you're making some for yourself,' I said.

'I am.' She turned without another word and went to the kitchen which, as the flat was identical to Trish's, I knew was next to the living room.

A couple of minutes passed. I could hear a faint clatter from the kitchen. She sneezed once. Outside, it started to rain. I sat for a while and watched the raindrops bounce off the window pane. It was heavy and I hoped it wouldn't last. I didn't relish the prospect of driving home in it.

Ten minutes later, Lesley still hadn't returned from the kitchen. I called her name. 'Lesley? Have you gone to China for that tea?' No reply. 'Hey, Lesley! Are you all right in there?'

Silence.

I got up from the sofa and went to the kitchen door, which was closed. I knocked. 'Lesley? Are you okay? Can I come in?'

Silence. Then a very muffled thud. And a whimper.

I opened the door and went in. She was sitting at the kitchen table, naked. She had a chopper in her right hand. Her left hand was flat on the table in front of her. She'd chopped off her thumb, index and middle fingers. They were in a neat row on the table, which was thick with dark blood.

She smiled at me. 'Your tea'll be ready soon.' She hacked off her third finger.

'Christ! Oh, Christ ...' I moved towards her.

'*Fuck off, you muck-raking cunt!*' She sprang from her stool and waved the chopper at me. Her face was grey. Her pimply, naked body was smeared with blood. '*Fuck off! Go home and have a wank before I cut your prick off!*'

'Lesley —' I broke off as she lunged, swinging the chopper at my head. I backed off, clenching a fist to hit her, but it wasn't necessary. As her blow missed me, she went with the swing and dropped to the floor.

'Christ ...' I kicked the chopper well away from her, then got a towel from a rail on the wall by the sink. Squatting next to the gibbering form on the floor, I

seized her left wrist and wrapped the towel round what was left of her hand.

'Leave me alone, you fucker.' Her voice was slurred and her eyes were closed. I lifted her from her floor with some difficulty (I'm not the strongest of guys – I look like the 'before' photo on a Charles Atlas advert) and carried her through to the living room, where I laid her on the sofa. She seemed to have passed out.

I picked up her phone and dialled 999. When the operator answered, I tried to speak, but all that came out was a frightened bleat. I tried again, and this time managed to ask for police and an ambulance.

I checked Lesley's hand. The towel was saturated with blood. I took off my belt and fastened it tightly round her wrist. She didn't wake up but distinctly mumbled the word 'Fucker.'

I rang Trish at work. 'Listen,' I said when she'd answered, 'don't, under *any* circumstances, come home tonight. In fact, don't come near Maryhill. Meet me in Café Oblomov at eight.'

'Why? What's up?'

'I'll tell you when I see you. But you're not coming back here.'

'Here? Where are you?'

'I'm in Maryhill,' I said. 'And I don't want you near it.'

'Gary, I *live* there. I'm not staying at your place tonight or –'

'*Listen*, you stupid bitch!' I exploded. 'I'm not fucking joking. You wouldn't *believe* what's going on up here.

Do you want to fucking die?'

'Wh-what?'

The doorbell rang. 'Look, I've got to go. Meet me in Oblomov at eight, right?'

'All right.' She sounded shaken. 'What do I do until eight?'

'I don't give a fuck. Just stay away from here.' I put the phone down and went to answer the door.

It was after six when I got away from Maryhill. It was raining hard. I got into my car and waved to the policemen as I drove off. I was crying with sheer horror.

I drove into town and wandered around for a while. My jacket and jeans were stained with Lesley's blood. I hadn't had a shower that day, and I smelled like a midden. I wanted to vomit but couldn't.

It was getting dark when I drove to my flat at around seven. It was still raining, though not as heavily. The street was empty. I sat in the car for a moment just looking out of the windows and feeling completely alone.

As I walked to my close, I realised there was somebody standing at the entrance. When I reached the close I saw that it was Glenn Lenzie.

'Gary, I want to talk to you,' he said as I tried to walk past him. He grabbed hold of my jacket, seeming not to notice the blood. 'I said I want to talk to you! I've been waiting for hours,' he whined.

I looked at him. I always found the sight of Lenzie revolting, but now he looked like a badly-assembled Guy Fawkes. It was as if he was just a head, and somebody had stuffed some clothes with rags and hung them on to the head. There was something oddly disturbing about the way he looked and, in my present frame of mind, it freaked me out.

'Glenn,' I said calmly, 'if you don't get away from here right now, I'm going to kick seven shades of shit out of you. I'm going to keep at it till I'm sure you'll never walk again. If you die, so much the better. And once I've finished, I'm going to call the police and get them to arrest what's left of you. I'll say you attacked me and I acted in self-defence. How'd you fancy that?'

Lenzie started to reply. I hit him hard in the mouth with my right fist. He gasped and sat down hard. 'You dirty cunt,' he said through a mouthful of blood.

'That felt good, you little fuckpig. If you don't piss off, I'll make myself feel great.'

He got up and shambled out of the close. I watched till I was certain he'd gone, then went up to my flat.

I stripped, and put my bloodstained clothes in the bin. Then I made some tea, and drank it huddled over the gas fire. The knuckles of my right hand ached.

I had a shower and put on fresh jeans and jumper. It was a quarter to eight. My feeling of horror had passed, leaving me now with a sensation of loneliness that, in its own way, was almost as bad.

I drove to Café Oblomov in Byres Road, near where I lived. It was an elegant café-bar, much loved by trendoids but pleasant nonetheless. Trish was sitting at a table on her own. I went over and sat down opposite her. 'Hi,' I said.

'You look terrible,' she said worriedly. She looked

great. She wore a smart blue suit, and her face glowed without the aid of make-up. She was fresh and vibrant and looking at her gave me a reminder of what I used to see in her.

'I feel terrible.' I smiled at her. 'You're the best thing I've seen all day.'

'So, what's happened?' she asked.

'Have you eaten?'

'Not yet,' she said.

'Let's have something to eat first,' I suggested. 'You don't want to hear this on an empty stomach.' We ordered baked potatoes with salad, and ate them in silence. Afterwards, we drank white wine and I told her what had happened to Lesley.

'She died while they were taking her down to the ambulance. Shock and loss of blood, I suppose. I'd to talk to the police for about two hours.'

'Excuse me.' As I'd guessed she might, Trish jumped up and headed for the toilet. She returned a few minutes later, not looking much better. 'I wasn't sick, but I thought I would be,' she said. She sat down and took a tentative sip of wine. 'Do the police think Lesley did the killing?' she asked.

'They're not sure. It's hard to imagine one woman being able to make such a mess of a body. In fact, it's hard to imagine five men being up to it.'

She looked at me. 'You don't think it was Lesley, do you?'

'No,' I said.

'But if she was crazy enough to cut her fingers off and try to kill you ...'

'I know. She was certainly capable of murder today. But I still don't think it was her. I don't think she killed the dog, and I certainly don't think she killed Clare Gibney. I don't see how she could've, for one thing.'

'What *do* you think, then?'

'I think she was driven out of her mind by what's happening up there. And I don't want you going near it till it's over. If it ever is. You know, the police are even scared. They haven't a clue what's going on.'

Trish fiddled with her signet ring. 'My God. My God.'

'So, like it or not, I want you to stay at my place. All right?'

She nodded. 'Okay.'

We went back to my flat at ten. I made tea for us both, and we sat together on the sofa, watching TV. 'What'll I do about a change of clothes?' she asked after a while.

'I'll go up to your place and get whatever you need tomorrow,' I said.

'All right.' She leaned her head on my shoulder. 'I think I'll have the day off work tomorrow,' she told me. 'I'll call in sick. I don't think I could face a class tomorrow.'

'Tell you what,' I said. 'If I'm not needed urgently at the mag, I'll take tomorrow off too. We can spend the day together.'

'Great.' She kissed me. It had been a long time since she'd last shown such genuine affection. I thought of Rhona and felt like a slug.

We went to bed at one in the morning. Neither of us

thought of making love. I'm ashamed to admit that, for reasons unknown, I felt oddly happy. I fell asleep in Trish's arms feeling that I was where I ought to be and everything might just be all right. And then ...

I had a dream that scared me too badly for it to be dismissed as a mere 'nightmare'. It pushed me uncomfortably close to the half-world of insanity that Lesley'd found her way into.

I was standing in a grey street in Maryhill. My mother stood at the entrance to a close. She'd no eyes. Her hands were thrust into the pockets of her shabby trenchcoat. Then she smiled at me, and took her hands from the pockets. Only she didn't have hands; she had two huge magnets instead of hands, and they dragged me irresistibly towards her. I screamed.

I was still screaming a minute later, when I was wide awake and the light was on and Trish was cuddling me and saying it was just a dream and not to be scared and I wasn't scared I was terrified.

# SIX

Considering what I'd been through, the way I felt the following day was ridiculous. Maybe danger makes you appreciate what you've got, I don't know. I only know that on that day, a Thursday, I felt happier and more content than I had in years.

I woke early and phoned Ian. 'Hi, it's Gary,' I said.

'What's up?' He spoke through a mouthful of food.

I told him of the previous afternoon's events. 'So, if you can survive without me, I'm taking today off. I need to relax for a bit.'

'Yeah.' He was shocked. 'Yeah. I'll look after things at the mag. You just take it easy.' He sounded worried. 'But, fuck's sake, Gary.' He paused, then, 'Are you okay?'

'I'm fine,' I said. 'I just want to wind down a bit.'

'If I'd seen what you saw, I'd be in a padded cell right now,' said Ian.

'Nah, I'm okay. It wasn't pretty, but I've seen worse things.' A lot worse, I thought. There's nothing like a Maryhill childhood to see to that.

'D'you reckon it was the girl who'd been doing all the hacking up?' Ian asked.

'No. I'm sure it wasn't. I'll talk to you about it later.

We'll have to run a heavy feature about it in next month's mag. I take it you haven't seen today's papers?'

'No, not yet. I'm not long up. Have you?'

'No, I'm just out of bed,' I told him. 'But I'd imagine they'll write it up pretty big. I'm just surprised I haven't had them on the blower wanting information.'

'You will,' said Ian.

'I know. Anyway, phone Jim Muriston at the *Glasgow Clarion*.' Muriston was a good friend and contact of mine who worked for Glasgow's foremost daily paper. 'Tell him to call me at home if he wants to know anything about yesterday. And tell him to let us know anything he hears about the case.'

'Okay.'

'Are you sure you can manage without me today?' I asked.

'Of course. Don't worry about anything. Just enjoy your day.'

'Thanks, Ian. I'll see you tomorrow.'

'Right. Call me if you need anything. Bye.'

'Bye.'

I put the phone down, struck suddenly by how good I was feeling. Outside there was a thin drizzle and a cruel wind, but I felt sunny. I felt then that if you're twenty-four, healthy, not starving, not in prison, and with a place to stay, then really you're okay. It wasn't that the creeping terror I'd felt had disappeared; it was just that I now felt able to face it.

I'd made the phone call from the living room. I went through to the bedroom, where Trish was still sleeping like a child. I got into bed and put my arms around her.

She woke, smiling sleepily. 'You're cold,' she said. 'I'll soon warm you, though.' And we lay holding each other for an hour.

Trish was dropping off to sleep when I kissed her lightly and said, 'It's ten o'clock. I'm going to get a paper and some breakfast for us, okay?'

She kissed me back. 'Okay.' As I got out of bed, she snuggled into the pillows and was asleep by the time I'd finished dressing.

I walked down to a newsagent's on Dumbarton Road and scanned the dailies on the shelf. The *Scotsman*, *Glasgow Herald* and *Glasgow Clarion* all had the murder of Clare Gibney and suicide of Lesley Tobin on the front page. All three mentioned that I'd been there, and the *Clarion* ran a small photo of me, which surprised me since they didn't have a quote.

I bought the *Clarion*, then went to a nearby dairy for milk, rolls and fruit. As I strolled back to my flat in the rain, I felt totally at peace with myself.

Trish was drinking a glass of orange juice and listening to the radio when I got back. 'Ian rang,' she told me. 'He said to tell you to expect the daily papers on the phone. They've all been ringing him at the office, wanting you, but he wouldn't give them your home number. He said they'd soon get it, though.'

'He's right.' My number's always been ex-directory, but that's no real problem to anybody who really wants to find you. I know; it's never stopped me.

Trish and I had breakfast and read the paper. The *Clarion* was the first of the dailies to ring me.

'Hello, Gary? It's Jim Muriston here. I called the

*Review*, and Ian said it was okay to call you at home.'

'Yes, it's fine. I take it you want to know about Lesley Tobin.'

'Uh-huh. I know you were there interviewing her, but what happened, Gary?'

I told him, leaving out the bit about her trying to kill me. I wanted to save that for my article in the next issue of the mag.

'Christ,' he said when I'd finished. 'What d'you make of it?'

'Nothing yet.'

'Oh, come on. You must have some feeling about it.'

'I've got feelings, yes. But no ideas.'

'You said in your mag editorial that the area is sick. D'you still feel that way?'

He was after a quote. Well, that was okay. It's a pain in the arse when your main witness doesn't say anything really quotable. I said, 'Okay, Jim. Here it comes – *Indeed I do still feel that way. Maryhill is diseased. It is now being consumed by some inexplicable, creeping disease that will eventually kill it. How many more deaths will it take before the authorities see that something must be done?* There, how's that?' I asked.

Muriston laughed. 'Great. Thanks, Gary.'

'No bother,' I said. 'Listen, Jim. If you hear anything else about this affair, give me a ring and let me know. The mag isn't due out for another month yet, so I won't be getting the jump on you. In return, I'll tell you anything I find out.' Well, almost anything.

'Okay, I will. Thanks again, Gary.' He hung up. I was

less helpful when the other dailies phoned, though I gave them a brief outline of what'd happened.

The rest of the day passed as though Maryhill and what was going on there were only inventions of a troubled mind. I drove up there to get the stuff Trish wanted from her flat – including about half of her wardrobe – and then almost forgot about the place for the rest of the day.

And it was like we were on holiday. In the afternoon we trailed around shops and coffee-houses, galleries and arcades in the West End. We went to an Indian restaurant for a meal at six in the evening, then went to the Citizens Theatre. We arrived back at my flat around ten-thirty, tired and like a couple of giggly children. I had never felt so close to Trish before. Surprisingly, I didn't think of Rhona once during the day, which doesn't say much for me, I suppose.

We made love that night and it was different from anytime before and I couldn't really understand it. And I fell asleep expecting the nightmare I'd had the previous night. I know I had some dream, and it wasn't pleasant, but I couldn't remember what it was about.

I wasn't feeling quite as great when I arrived at the mag the next morning, but I still felt pretty fine. That didn't last long.

Ian had a face like a knife as he came into my office a few minutes after I'd arrived. 'How're you feeling?' he asked morosely.

'Not so bad, considering everything. What's up?'

'I got some news last night, but I didn't want to bother you with it then ...'

'What is it?'

'Glenn's dead.'

'How? When?' I said disbelievingly.

'Last night.'

'What happened?'

'He was in a pub in Possil. He was drunk. He dug some guy up, started a fight with him. The guy pulled a blade, and that was the end of Glenn.'

'What ... the guy killed him?'

'Yes. Cut his throat. He was dead when the police got there,' said Ian. Seeing my expression he added, 'Don't start feeling guilty. What you did to him was perfectly in order.'

'I know. But still. Fuck's sake!'

'Gary, the guy was a loser. He was a self-pitying, malicious little shit. The fact that he's dead doesn't change that.'

I sat back in my chair and closed my eyes for a few seconds. 'I know. You're right.'

'The pigs want someone from the mag to go down to the morgue and identify the body,' said Ian. 'The only family he had was a sister in London, and they can't find her. Shall I go?'

I thought about it. I've got a far stronger stomach than Ian. In fact, I've got a stronger stomach than anyone I've ever known. 'No. I'll go. I'll head down there later this morning.'

Ian looked concerned. 'Are you sure?'

'Uh-huh. Don't worry. Stiffs don't bother me much.'

I phoned Raymond at home. I had to let it ring for five minutes before he answered with a groggy 'H'lo?'

'Hi, Raymond, my dutiful, beautiful photographer. How's life?'

'Okay. You woke me up,' he grumbled.

'Sorry about that. But, you remember I told you to take a week off?'

'Yeah. You want me to come in?'

'No, don't worry. But I'll need you to stand by. Have you read about the murder in Maryhill?'

'Nah. Haven't read the papers for ages.'

'Well, I'll tell you about it later. I might need you to take some photos of some of the people involved in the investigation. So you may have to cut your holiday short.'

'Don't worry, it's cool. Just ring me if you need me.'

'Thanks. I'll let you get back to bed now. And, Raymond – ?'

'Yeah?'

'Read a paper, you ignorant bastard.' He was laughing when I hung up.

I looked at my watch. Almost ten. I went through to the main office, where Ian sat reading a copy of the *Glasgow Clarion*. On the front page was Jim Muriston's article, with a quote from me and a photo taken a couple of years ago, in which I looked like Norman Bates. 'The *Clarion*'s taking this seriously,' Ian said.

'They're right to,' I told him. 'Look, I'm going to head down to the morgue now. Is there anything you need before I go?'

'Rhona's supposed to be working today, but she

hasn't shown. D'you know anything about it?' he asked.

I shook my head. 'Phone her and find out what's happened to her. Anything else?'

'Paul Campbell's having a press conference this morning, at eleven. D'you want someone to go along?'

'Go along yourself. Take a note of anything the crooked bastard says. We'll be sure to write it up next issue.'

'We'll *both* end up in jail this time,' Ian muttered as I left.

I went for a piss. As I washed my hands afterwards, I looked in the toilet's grimy mirror. It was weird, but I'd never looked so healthy. Normally, I look as though I've just got out of a coffin, but on that day I was radiant. There was colour in my cheeks, my eyes were bright, I had a few days' growth of beard, and I looked pretty good.

Glenn's corpse didn't. As dead people go, he had very clearly gone. The morgue attendant, thinking me a friend of Lenzie's (note the strange temptation to call people you hated by their first names after they die), had told me to prepare for a shock before he opened the drawer containing the stiff.

Lenzie wasn't the most handsome guy when he was alive, and being dead didn't improve him any. His assailant had actually cut him from ear to ear, and I think he must have lost every drop of blood in his body. His skin was pure white, and he seemed to have physically shrunk. He was still a misshapen blob, but now he somehow seemed a much smaller blob. His face still wore the cruel, petty look that had endeared him to so many during his lifetime. He wasn't an appealing sight. If I'd ever been into necrophilia, Lenzie's corpse would have put me off.

I identified the stiff, signed the piece of paper the attendant gave me, and left. The morgue was in Glasgow's notorious East End, so I felt relieved to find my car still in one piece.

Poor Lenzie, I thought as I drove back to the office. I wondered if anybody could ever deserve what he'd copped. I'm still not sure of the answer.

I stopped for a cup of tea in a little café not far from the office. I was beginning to feel lethargic, and couldn't be arsed working. For half an hour I sat at a table next to the window and watched the rain fall outside. Finally, I stirred myself and went back to the mag.

Ian had gone to the Paul Campbell press conference. I asked Heather if he'd left any messages. 'Uh-huh.' She nodded. 'He called Rhona to find out why she wasn't at work. She wouldn't tell him, said she'd speak to you later.'

'Oh. Okay.' That puzzled me. It didn't sound good.

'And some guy phoned to complain about your *Maryhell* article. He says it's a hatchet job on the area. Says he's coming down here to kill you.'

'Did he say when?'

'No. I offered him an appointment, but he didn't take it.' She looked at me, hesitated, then said, 'Did you see Glenn's body?'

'Uh-huh. Not very nice.' I went to my office before

she could ask any more about it.

I phoned Rhona. Her mother answered, and demanded to know who I was. Surprised by her aggressive tone, I said, 'It's Gary Scott. Her editor. She didn't come in to work today. Is she all right?'

'Hold on. I'll get her,' Attila the Mum said grudgingly. A minute later, Rhona said hello in an odd voice.

'Hi, Rhona, it's Gary. What's the matter?'

'I can't come in to work,' she said. Her voice was *weird*. I didn't like it at all.

'Well, okay. When will you be in?'

'Gary, I'm not going to work for the *Review* any more.' I suddenly realised she was crying.

'How come? You've only just started.' I was trying to keep my tone light.

'I've decided not to go out with you any more. I can't finish with you and go on working for you.'

'Why not? And why're you finishing with me?'

'My head's really in a mess, Gary. I need some time to myself.'

'Why? What's up?'

'Peter asked me to go out with him last night. I said no, and he broke my arm.'

I said nothing for a few seconds, feeling my eyes water the way they always do on the occasions when I'm dangerously angry. 'Where does he live?' I finally asked.

'Stop it, Gary. I'm not going to tell you where he lives, and I'm not going to listen to you if you're going to be stupid.'

'All right.' I was tapping my foot on the floor and my

body was trembling slightly. 'But I want to see you.'

'You can't.'

'*Why?*'

'I told you, I want some time to myself. I don't want to see Peter, or you. I love him and ...' She sniffled for a moment. 'Besides, you're not Jewish.'

'So what? I'm not proposing marriage.'

'I know, but ... Look, Gary, just fuck off!' She put the phone down.

I called back immediately. Her mother answered. 'Rhona doesn't want to speak to you,' she told me.

'Tell her she'd better, or I'll come over there and speak to her face to face,' I told her.

Rhona came on. 'What is it?' Her voice was thick.

'Look, I don't mind if you don't want to go out with me again,' I said. 'But if you should decide you want your job again, all you have to do is phone me and we'll find something for you. Right?'

'Thanks, Gary. I'm sorry I swore at you.'

'Don't worry, I'm used to it.'

'Thanks.'

'Promise you'll ring me if you want the job?'

'I will.'

'Okay. Now take it easy. Bye.'

I had a mug of tea and cooled down. Considering the way things seemed to be going between Trish and me, I wasn't too bothered by Rhona's not wanting to go out with me any more. But the idea of some fuckpig injuring her turned my guts.

The phone rang. I picked it up. 'Scott.'

'It's Jim Muriston here, Gary.'

76

'Oh, hi. I read today's *Clarion*. Did you have to use that photo of me? I look like Norman Bates.'

'Gary, have you heard anything from Maryhill today?'

I froze. 'No. What's happened?'

'I'm not really sure, the story's just come in – '

'*What* story, Jim?'

'I'm telling you. That kid who was murdered, Clare Gibney – her parents killed themselves. They've just been found. That's all I know right now. I'll ring you as soon as I find out more.'

'Make sure you do.'

'Hold on, Gary!' he said with sudden anger. 'I'm doing you a favour. I'm not a fucking news agency. You can give me orders when you start paying me.'

He was right, of course. 'I'm sorry, Jim. I'm really uptight about this story.'

He laughed, his anger gone as suddenly as it'd come. 'It's okay. I'll call you later.' He rang off.

I'd just put the phone down when it rang again. 'Scott.'

It was Heather, ringing through from the main office. 'There's a Constable Jamieson here asking to see you. He says it's important.'

'Send him through.'

'Okay. D'you want tea or coffee?'

'I'll have a cup of tea. Ask him what he wants.'

A moment later there was a knock on my door, and Perky entered. He was in plain clothes, and he looked as if he'd aged ten years.

'Hi, Constable. Have a seat,' I said brightly. He sat

down without a word. His expression didn't change. 'What can I do for you?' I asked.

'Nothing, really,' he said. 'I've just come to tell you a few things, Mr Scott. Just some things you might want to know.' At that moment Heather arrived with tea for me and coffee for Perky. He took it from her with a listless nod.

'So what is it?' I asked him when Heather'd gone.

'I have to make something clear first,' said Perky. 'If you ever tell anybody what I'm going to tell you, I'll deny it. If you publish it, I'll sue you for malicious libel.'

'All right. What is it?'

'Promise you'll never repeat it?'

'If I do, I won't mention your name,' I assured him.

'Right.' For a moment he sipped his coffee and said nothing. Then, 'I might as well tell you that I won't be on duty in Maryhill anymore. I've told my sergeant I'll pack in the job before I'll work there again, after last night.'

'What happened last night?'

He went on as if he hadn't heard me. 'I'm taking three weeks' holiday. I'm not due it, but I need it after last night. They can sack me if they like ...'

'What happened?' I said again.

'Last night, I paid a routine visit to Brian and Margaret Gibney. The dead kid's parents.'

'I know.'

'They'd been staying with friends. They just got back last night. I thought it best to check they were all right.' He hesitated.

'Uh-huh?' I prompted.

79

'So I went to see them. They seemed not too bad, considering what's happened to them. Coping quite well. You know.' Another hesitation.

'Constable, what happened?'

It all came in a rush then. 'They've got another kid, about six months old. A baby.' He used the present tense, so he obviously hadn't found out about their deaths. 'The baby was sleeping in a cot in the living room, where we all were. At one point, the parents went to the kitchen to make us all a snack. While they were gone, the baby sat up in the cot, smiled at me, and said "Get out of here, you fucking woman-killer."' Perky sat glaring at me. 'You can laugh now.'

'I'm not going to laugh,' I told him.

'If you believe me, you're as mental as I am!'

'I'm not saying I believe you. I said I'm not going to laugh at you,' I told him. 'It's not funny when you consider that the parents – and maybe the kid, I don't know yet – were found dead this morning.'

'*What?*'

'Yes. I heard just before you got here. I assumed you didn't know.'

'I didn't. I didn't. Oh, *fuck* –'

'Are you okay?'

He stood up. 'I'm fine. I wish I was surprised. Oh, I really need to get out of here!' He was about to leave when he suddenly said, 'Can I ask your age, Mr Scott?'

'I'm twenty-four,' I answered, surprised. 'Why?'

'Well, you may think you're all man. You probably think you're wise to it all. Christ, I did. But you're still just a snotty-nosed wee boy.'

'What are you –'

'Listen. I'm not as smart as you, but I'm older. Stay away from Maryhill. Just drop the whole thing. Go and find a girl to screw, or something. Let it go. It's good being twenty-four.' He went out.

I called after him. He came back into the office. 'Why did that – baby call you a "woman-killer"?' I asked.

'Three years ago, a woman I arrested died in custody. I didn't touch her, but there was an inquiry. I was cleared, but a lot of people still think I was responsible.' His eyes were wet. 'I don't care how good you think you are, Mr Scott. If you want to fuck with whatever's doing this, you're going to need a big dick.'

'I've got one,' I said. Perky smiled sickly as he left.

I didn't do any work that afternoon. Jim Muriston phoned back, to tell me that the baby'd been found dead as well. The parents had cut their own wrists and the baby's throat.

I just sat staring at my desk. It was getting heavy. Like I said, I've got a strong stomach, but three suicides and two murders in one week are a bit much. Three murders, if you include an unrelated one. Lenzie's. *One I knew I was indirectly to blame for.* Heavy.

Ian should've been back from the Paul Campbell press conference around two, but it was four-fifteen when he walked into my office. 'What held you up? I was beginning to think somebody'd topped you as well,' I said sourly.

'There was a delay in the conference starting. What's up?'

I told him about the suicides. When I said they'd killed the baby too, he looked ill. Then I told him Perky's story. 'You're kidding!' he said incredulously, starting to laugh. Then he saw my expression and stopped laughing. 'Gary! You actually believe him, don't you?' He was horrified.

Now I did laugh. 'No, not quite. But I'm past taking the piss out of anything.' I thought for a moment, then said, 'If there's anywhere a six-month-old baby could talk, and curse at you, then that's the place.'

Ian sat down. 'I'll tell you something,' he said. 'I'll tell you what you should do right now. For the rest of this month, until the next issue's out, you should stay away from this office. Just forget magazine business. Forget anything to do with journalism. The mag won't fall apart 'cause you're not here for a month. I muddled by as acting editor when you were in jail. I can do it again.'

I shook my head. 'You think I've flipped, don't you?'

'No, or I'd be telling you to see a shrink. But I don't think your judgement's at its best-ever. You've had a few shocks over the past week. I think you should have a rest or you *might* flip.'

'You might not be all that far wrong,' I admitted. 'But I can't opt out of this one.'

'You're fucking obsessed.'

'I know. But I still can't let this go. I'll take a holiday after the next issue comes out.'

'Promise?' Ian demanded.

'You've got it. I promise, you won't see me for at

least a month.' I grinned at him. 'And if I don't like the mag you bring out, you're fired.'

Ian laughed. 'Nah. I'm planning a mutiny. I might just get to like being editor too much to give it up.'

We spent what remained of the working day drinking tea and talking. I expected an interrogation when I told him Rhona wouldn't be working for the mag anymore, but he only nodded and said, 'Oh.'

At five, I rang my flat. Trish answered. 'Hi, it's Gary,' I said.

'Hello.' She sounded fairly bright. 'How's your day been?'

'Lots happening. I'll explain later. How about yours?'

'Terrible. I'm coming to realise that teaching's probably not for me!' she said laughing.

'Have you heard the news from Maryhill yet?'

'No, what news?'

'I'll tell you later. I just called to tell you I won't be straight home. There's something I want to do first.'

'Oh, okay. When will you be home?'

'In an hour or so.'

'Okay. Are you all right? You sound weird.'

'I'm fine. See you later.'

# SEVEN

I didn't really have anything to do after work. I just wanted to be on my own for a while. For reasons I still don't understand, I headed my car in the direction of Maryhill.

It was daylight, but the place gave the impression of being dark, as it always did for me. For a while I just drove around. It was raining – as it usually is during the Scottish summer – and there weren't many people on the dirty streets. I saw a bunch of kids, aged about eight or nine, sheltering in a pub doorway. They wore grubby anoraks and trousers – even the girls. They were laughing and shouting, and I wondered how long it'd be before that area stifled their laughter forever. If you're born in a place like that, you do one of three things: get out, go insane or, worst of all, become part of it.

Maybe it was the sight of the kids that made me drive over to Hunterdunn Street, where I was born. Where I hadn't been since I was fourteen. *Ten years. Jesus.*

The street hadn't changed much. The Bogey Close was still there. I got out of my car and went to look at it. It was still the same.

It was called the Bogey Close. All the grown-ups called it that when speaking to us kids. It was where the Bogey Man was supposed to live. You could understand why it was that close and not any of the four others on the block. It was always pitch dark, having no windows and a faulty gas lamp. When I was eight years old, I experienced the thrill of running through the Bogey Close, a feat that earned you the kids' equivalent of the Victoria Cross, such was the courage it was thought to require. You'd enter from the street, running hard even as you approached the dark mouth of the close. Then you'd plunge into the blackness and begin a journey that lasted ten seconds but seemed to go on forever. You'd hear the pounding of your feet on the stone floor as you ran, expecting at any moment a pair of cold, wet hands to grab you. Then, just as you thought your legs were going to give out and you were going to be sick and you were going to be there in the darkness forever, the darkness would spit you out into the grey daylight of the back court, where your friends would be waiting to see whether you'd make it or whether the Bogey Man would get you.

Nobody lived in the Bogey Close, if you exclude the Bogey Man. Only one of the flats was ever occupied that I remember. The tenant was an old woman named Mrs Monstroe, locally known as Mrs Monster. One night she cut out her own tongue. They carted her off to hospital, and that was the last that anyone saw of her. If there were ever any more occupants of the close, I don't remember them.

It was the accepted wisdom among the kids that, if you were alone in the back court at night, you'd hear the Bogey Man's song coming from the close. We used to sing it to each other on long summer evenings and scare ourselves shitless. It was an eerie chant which went:

*I'm the Bogey, Bogey,*
*I'm the Bogey Man.*
*I'm there when it gets dark,*
*To kill you if I can.*

And once, in broad daylight, I was in the back court and heard it. And, as only a child could, I just ignored it and went on playing in a dirty puddle.

For a long time I stood leaning on the bonnet of my car, looking at the Bogey Close and half-expecting to hear that chant again. But of course I didn't. I'm a big boy now.

The rain became heavier. I got back in my car and drove away from Hunterdunn Street. A few minutes of aimless driving brought me to Maryhill Road, the area's centre. I pulled up outside a small café, sat in my car for a while, then stirred myself. I went into the café and bought a cheese roll and a can of coke.

The place was dirty and deserted, but strangely, frighteningly welcoming. There was a sick smell, a smell of coming home. I felt torn as I went out into the rain; part of me wanted to stay in the café, the rest of me

87

couldn't wait to get out.

I was about to get into my car when I saw a dosser approaching, dragging his feet in a sort of Frankenstein walk. I put the food I'd bought into my car, then fumbled in my pocket for loose change. There was nothing but a few coppers. For no reason I know of, I took a fiver from my wallet, walking to meet the old guy as I did. 'Here.' I held it out to him.

'You're a champion, son.' He took the money from me. He was caked with mud and smelled like a toilet. His filthy hair was so long I couldn't see his eyes.

'You're welcome. Take it easy.' I turned to get into my car. I was already so wet that my jeans were plastered to my legs.

'Don't come back here,' he said.

'What?' I looked at him and saw nothing.

'Don't come back. It's dark here.' I still couldn't see his eyes.

'What did you say?' My voice shook.

'You know what I said. Gary. It's dark here. Gary. There's no light.'

When he said my name, I felt as though icy water was running down my legs, and wondered vaguely if I'd wet myself, knowing at the same time I hadn't.

'There's light sometimes,' I heard myself blurt, then I was in my car, frantically trying to start it. Then I was driving away, out of Maryhill, and the car was rotten with the stink of my fear.

At ten that night, I was still driving around. I thought of how good it would be to drive into the countryside, into the darkness. *It's dark here. Gary.*

*There's no light.* It'd be so good to just go, just lose myself in the rainy darkness. *It's dark here. Gary.*

Gary.

I thought of how good it'd be, then went home.

# EIGHT

When I walked into my living room, Trish was sitting on the sofa, in her dressing-gown. Her face was pale and tight. 'Where've you been?' she said in a brittle voice.

'Just wandered,' I mumbled, taking off my jacket. Trish came to me, without warning, and clung to me convulsively, pressing her face to my neck. I was so numb mentally that it was a moment before I realised that she was crying.

'C'mon.' I held her gently, stroking her hair. 'Don't, Trish. I'm okay, honest. I'm sorry I was late. I'm sorry I worried you.' She hiccupped something I couldn't make out and went on crying. 'Trish . . .'

*Gary.*

'Trish, I'm okay.' She didn't answer, but after a while her crying subsided. I pushed her face away from my neck, tilted her chin and looked at her. Her face was red and puffy and tearstained and lovely. She didn't speak.

I grinned at her, trying to make it look genuine. 'How about a smile?' I asked. She shook her head, looking like she'd cry again.

For no reason at all, I suddenly felt like crying

myself. I closed my eyes and swallowed it down, then opened them and said, 'Listen. You sit down and I'll go and make you a coffee, okay?' Wordlessly, she nodded. 'Good.' I sat her down on the sofa and grinned again. 'D'you think I'd let anything happen to me while I've got somebody like you to come back to?' I said lamely, and was rewarded with a feeble smile.

I went to the kitchen and made coffee for Trish and tea for myself, then brought it to the living room and set it on the table in front of the sofa. I sat beside Trish and put an arm around her. 'All right now?' I asked.

She nodded solemnly. 'Uh-huh.'

'Give me another smile, then.' She did.

We hugged each other in silence for a moment, then she said, 'Where did you go?'

'Up to Maryhill.'

She looked sick. 'I knew it. What did you do?'

'Just drove around. Don't worry.'

I stretched out on the sofa with my head in Trish's lap. I took off my glasses and closed my eyes. I had the feeling of waking from a nightmare, of getting back in touch with the real world, with its reassuring everyday misery.

'Ian phoned,' said Trish, stroking my hair. 'He said Paul Campbell phoned him, threatening to sue about some article. Ian said you'd understand.'

'He can sue and be damned.'

I yawned.

'And a guy called Glenn phoned.'

'*Who?*'

'Glenn. Didn't say what his second name was. He

92

said to tell you he's holding out over his article about the Bogey Close.'

Later, I phoned Ian. Not right away, of course. First I went to the bedroom, buried my face in the pillow and screamed for a long time. When I wouldn't tell Trish why, she insisted I call Ian or she'd call a doctor.

I made Trish go to the bedroom while I phoned Ian from the living room. 'Why? Gary, what are you hiding?' she asked desperately. She looked terrified and I wanted to tell her, but I knew the truth would scare her even worse, whether she believed it or not.

'I'll tell you soon. I promise. Go on.' She went to the bedroom and I called Ian.

It was some time before he answered with a groggy 'Hello?'

'Hi, it's Gary.'

'Gary? What time is it?'

'Two in the morning. Sorry I woke you, Ian. I had to talk to you.'

'What's up? Don't tell me somebody else's been killed!'

'No, it might be worse than that. I got home late tonight and –'

'I know. I rang you, and Trish answered,' he told me.

'Guess who else called while I was out?' Before he'd a chance to guess, I told him. 'Glenn Lenzie.'

A sigh. Then, 'Glenn's dead, Gary. You should know. You saw the corpse this morning.'

'I know I did. But being dead doesn't seem to stop him from phoning me.' I shocked myself by giggling suddenly.

'*Stop that!*' Ian snapped. 'Listen, you idiot. Glenn's *dead*. Whoever phoned, it wasn't him.'

'Who was it, then?'

'How do I know? It could've been any sick bastard. You've got a lot of enemies. You know that. Any of them could've heard about what happened to Glenn and phoned to wind you up.'

'I thought about that too, Ian. Except for the message he left with Trish. He said he was *holding out*. That was his catch-phrase, remember?'

'I know, it was practically his war cry,' said Ian. 'And he said it so often that anybody could've heard it and used it to give you a scare.'

'He also talked about something I was thinking about earlier tonight. Something nobody but me knows about. Something from when I was a kid.'

'Gary, you sound like you're raving. D'you want me to come over?'

'No, it's okay. I've got Trish here.'

'I think you ought to take that break we talked about. You're going to crack up if you don't.'

*It's dark here.*

'I can't. I said I couldn't let this one go. Now I don't think it'll let me go.'

*Gary.*

'Look, go to bed. I'll phone you in the morning. But at least go away for the weekend. It's Friday – well, Saturday now, I suppose. Go away till Monday. Please.'

'I'll think about it. In fact, I probably will. Thanks, Ian.'

'I'll talk to you tomorrow. Bye.'

I went through to the bedroom. Trish was lying in bed, restlessly flipping through a copy of the *City Review*. 'I spoke to Ian,' I told her. 'I'm okay now. Ian reckons I need a break. D'you fancy going away for the weekend?'

'Where to?'

'Not far. I want to be at work on Monday.'

'So will I.'

'All right, how about going through to Edinburgh? We could stay with Mark and Kerry, and come back late Sunday night.'

'Okay. Great. What time'll we leave?' she asked.

'First thing, almost. I'll make a few calls, then we'll get going.'

And that's what I did. Funnily enough, after my waking nightmare, I slept like the dead that night (although dead people of my acquaintance didn't seem to be particularly restful) and woke at eight in morning. I called Ian, getting him out of bed again, and told him of my decision to go to Edinburgh.

'Good,' he said. 'When're you coming back?'

'Sunday night. I'm only going for the weekend.'

'Better than nothing, I suppose. How d'you feel about last night now?'

I considered. 'Well, in daylight it seems really ridiculous. But I can't think of any explanation for what happened. Whoever it was on the phone knew things that nobody but me could know.'

'But come on. D'you think Glenn was so pissed off at your sacking him that his ghost's phoning you up?'

I laughed. 'I know how it sounds. I'll have a think

about it over the weekend. But a lot of weird things're happening.'

'Well, try and take it easy. Who're you going to stay with – Mark?'

'Uh-huh.'

'Well, say hello for me.'

'I will. Thanks, Ian. I hope my head'll be straighter by Monday.'

'So do I. See you then.'

Ian hung up. Trish handed me a mug of tea as I dialled Mark Allen's number. Mark was deputy editor of *The Scene*, an Edinburgh events guide. Both Mark and his girlfriend Kerry, who he lived with, had worked for the *City Review* when I first got it going. They'd moved to Edinburgh the following year, and ever since then Mark had periodically called me to suggest that we set up a magazine together. I always declined; I liked the *Review* too much.

'Hello, Mark,' I said when he answered the phone. 'Gary Scott here.'

'Gaz! I was just talking about you last night. How's life?'

'Weird. Haven't you heard I've taken up finding dead bodies?'

'Eh?'

'You can't have been reading the papers, Mark.'

'No, I haven't. Kerry and I've been on holiday. Sweden. Just got back yesterday morning. Why, what's happening?'

'I'll tell you when I see you. I'm coming through to

Edinburgh today. Can you put me up for the night?'

'Of course. Will you be on your own?'

'No, Trish's coming too. Is that okay?'

'Fine. I'll be glad to see you both. So will Kerry.'

'How's Kerry doing?' I asked.

'Oh, she's doing. What time'll you be here at?'

'We're leaving in about half an hour,' I said.

'Great. See you later, then.' He rang off.

Trish and I caught a train to Edinburgh from Queen Street Station at nine-thirty. It was the first reasonably sunny day of the summer and a lot of people had taken it into their heads to go to Edinburgh. If we'd boarded the train a minute later, we wouldn't have got seats. As it happened, we were just in time to get a couple of seats facing each other over a table by the window.

As the train moved out of Glasgow, we sat in silence and watched fields drift by the window. I'd done it so many times before, made this boring hour-long journey to the capital surrounded by bored businessmen, bored husbands, bored wives, bored kids. The heat was stifling and a woman came through with a trolley selling nauseating British Rail refreshments and kids were whining and couples were falling out and it was all so beautifully *normal* ...

Usually, I found the journey – any journey, in fact – irritating, but now I just looked around me and enjoyed it. This was the best world to be in, though you didn't know till you were out of it for a while. In this world you occupied yourself with being unhappy about your job, miserable about your love life, or just depressed about everything. You didn't have dossers call you by your name and speak your worst fear, tell you about the darkness you'd tried not to even think about since you were a kid. You didn't have dead men read your mind and phone you up to tell you what you'd been thinking.

In this world, you knew such things couldn't happen. And I knew Ian'd been right and I needed this break or I might start believing in such things.

'Christ, it's stifling,' said Trish. Her face was red and sticky. 'I told you we should've taken the car.'

'Nah. The car'd have been as bad. And I'm too wound up to drive,' I told her. 'I'm actually enjoying this.'

'You must be nuts,' she said affectionately, and I reflected that she might not be wrong.


Trish and I arrived at Mark Allen's Marchmont flat at a quarter to eleven. Kerry opened the door just as I started to ring the bell.

'Hi!' She smiled. 'I saw you from the window. Come on in.' We followed her through the hall to the living room. She was a cheerful, tousle-haired girl of twenty-three, so manic that she always seemed ready to start jumping up and down as she spoke.

Mark was sitting on the floor in the cluttered living room, watching TV. In physical appearance, Mark and Kerry looked more like brother and sister than lovers. He was almost exactly like Kerry, but male.

'*Gaz!*' he burst out, getting to his feet as we came in.

'And the lovely Trish! How's things, babes?'

Trish just smiled and said nothing. She liked Mark, but found his hyperactiveness a bit overwhelming. 'Like I said on the blower, things're weird,' I told him, dropping my overnight bag on the floor.

Kerry nodded. 'We know. Mark went and got some of last week's papers after you phoned, just to see what you were on about.'

'Sounds hairy,' said Mark. 'How many stiffs've you been involved with?'

'I was only actually on the scene of one of them,' I said, sitting on the sofa. Trish sat down beside me. 'But you're right — it's hairy.'

Mark made some tea and I told him and Kerry some of what'd been going on, leaving out the weirder bits. It was really just a more detailed version of what they'd seen in the papers, I suppose.

'So, who d'you think's doing it?' Mark asked when I'd finished.

The answer could've got me detained under the Mental Health Act, so I just said, 'I haven't a clue, and neither have the police. I just had to get away from it for a while, which is what I'm doing here.'

'You know you're both welcome to stay as long as you like,' said Kerry.

'I know. Thanks. But we'll have to leave tomorrow night,' I said.

Mark looked at his watch. 'It's noon. I'm going to have to nip down to *The Scene* office for half an hour.'

I looked at him curiously. 'Working on a Saturday?' Mark was so lazy by nature, he made me look like a demon of industry.

'Got to. We go to press on Monday,' he said. 'I just want to take a look in and see how things're going. Paul, the editor, is on holiday, so I'll have to keep an eye on things. Want to come along?'

'Okay.' I've never been able to refuse an invitation to a magazine office around deadline. The frenzied tapping of typewriters and the sound of people shouting at each other have a compulsion I can neither understand nor resist.

'I'll stay here with Kerry,' said Trish.

The offices of *The Scene* were about ten minutes walk from Mark's flat. As we walked, he said, 'I don't suppose there's any point in asking if you've changed your mind about setting up together?'

I smiled and shook my head. 'Nothing's changed, Mark. It's a great idea, but it wouldn't work. I'd want to be editor and so would you —'

'Have two editors, then. Be innovative.'

'Who'd have the final say in decisions, then? You'd want it liberal and I'd want it left. Where you'd want it trendy, I'd want it hip. It'd be doomed. We're good mates, Mark. We wouldn't be a week after we set up together.'

'Okay.' He shrugged. 'I didn't think you'd changed your mind. I only asked 'cause there's obviously something wrong with you. I thought maybe you weren't happy with the *Review*.'

'What d'you mean, there's obviously something wrong?'

He said nothing for a moment, then told me, 'This photographer I knew committed suicide a couple of months ago. Before he did, he'd this sort of look about him. I can't describe it. He'd never looked so healthy, he was like – *radiant*. But his manner was weird. I can't pin it down, but you've got the same look about you.'

I forced a laugh. 'Don't get paranoid. The past week's been pretty stressful, that's all. I'm not planning to top myself.'

'If you do, I'll never speak to you again,' he said.

The weekend did what it was supposed to do, I think. It was like taking a bath in normality to wash away the nightmare of the past couple of days.

When Mark and I got back to his flat, Kerry and Trish suggested going for a walk. So for most of the day the four of us just drifted around the city centre, went shopping, strolled in parks, sat in bars. In the evening we had dinner in Henderson's, a popular vegetarian restaurant, then went back to the flat. Kerry got out her guitar and Mark opened a couple of bottles of wine, and we all got a little pissed and I played the guitar and we all sang until the early hours of Sunday morning.

Mark and Kerry folded down the living-room sofa to make a bed for Trish and me. After they'd gone to their bedroom we made love with our hands over each other's mouths to suppress first our giggles, then our groans.

It was three o'clock on Sunday afternoon before any of us woke. We had something to eat, then went to a cinema. Mark and Kerry saw us to our train at ten that night, promising to come to visit us soon.

The carriage was empty except for Trish and me. We

sat and held hands and looked out of the window into the night.

*It's dark here.*

As we neared Glasgow I felt like a man being drawn back to his mother and turned into a baby again and sucked back into the womb.

# NINE

'How're you feeling?' asked Ian, coming into my office on Monday morning.

'Not so bad,' I said, and it was true; I did feel pretty good. I was sitting at my desk with a cup of tea in front of me, and felt so normal. I felt like I was Gary Scott, editor of the *City Review*, at his desk on a Monday morning, a feeling I hadn't really had since Clare Gibney's murder.

'How'd your weekend go?' Ian sat on the edge of my desk.

'Fine. As usual, Mark wants me to set up a mag with him.'

'I wish you would, then I'd have this one,' he said.

The phone rang. 'Gary, there's a Peter Lewis here asking to see you,' said Heather. 'Says he's something to do with Rhona Jacobs.'

Peter. Rhona's boyfriend. Just what I was in the mood for. I grinned into the phone. 'Send him in.' I looked at Ian. 'Can you excuse me a while? It's personal.'

'Okay.' He left as my visitor came in.

Peter Lewis was a stocky, sharp-featured, curly-haired man in his late twenties. He wore designer jeans, a leather jacket and an angry look. 'You're Scott?'

'Mr Scott,' I said evenly.

He looked around the office with contempt. 'God, what a hovel.'

'You can get out of it, then. What d'you want?'

'You've been screwing my bird.'

'Depends on who she is.'

'Rhona.'

'Rhona who?' I said in the most infuriating manner I could assume.

'Rhona Jacobs. I'm her boyfriend.'

'Oh. You mean you're the bit of breathing sewage who broke her arm. Yes, I've been fucking her. I would again, given half a chance. What of it?' I taunted. He just glared. 'She gives great head,' I told him.

That did it. He came at me, swinging a right. Still in my chair, I kicked him hard in the knee as he came within range. He squealed and stumbled forward as I got up. He fell against me, hands grabbing for my throat. He was strong, but soft with wealth, and had no idea about fighting. I ripped two punches to his body, one of them going into his liver with a force that almost made me wince. As he fell, I let him have a right to the side of the head to see that he stayed down.

The door opened. 'What's going on?' demanded Ian, looking at the sobbing, crumpled figure on the floor.

'It's okay. Go,' I said. He did. I opened a drawer of my desk, and got out the replica revolver I kept there. It looked just like the real thing. (I didn't dare have a real gun; with a temper like mine, I'd've been locked up for murder in no time.)

I stood over Peter. 'Get up,' I said. He looked up and I pointed my toy at him. 'Get up before I air-condition your head.'

'I can't, you bastard. You've broken my ribs,' he wheezed.

'Anything you say,' I said, and cocked the pistol.

'All right!' His ribs miraculously healed themselves and he got to his feet.

I pressed the 'gun' to his forehead and smiled. 'Don't,' was all he could say as he began to shake.

'Why not? You attacked me. I can kill you and say it was self-defence. Or maybe I could just shoot your hands off. How many women's arms d'you reckon you could break then?'

His face twitched. 'Please.'

Suddenly, I was tired of the game. 'Get out of here. Come back and I'll squeeze what'll be left of you through the keyhole.'

'What happened there?' asked Ian, after Peter had limped out of the office.

'Rhona's boyfriend,' I said shortly.

'Oh. Thought it was a recalcitrant interviewee,' he said and we both laughed.

Ian went back through to the main office, and I sat on my own for a while. I couldn't believe how polished my fighting skills had been. Other than the punch in the mouth I'd given Glenn Lenzie, I hadn't been involved in a violent incident for years. I couldn't help but think of where I'd learned to fight.

*Stop it, you idiot. Fighting's like riding a bike. It's there for life.*

I called Rhona's number. 'Hi, it's Gary Scott. How're you doing?'

'All right. What's the matter?'

'I've just had your boyfriend over here, trying to do me.'

'Christ! Are you all right?'

'Fine. I can't speak for him, though. He wasn't up to it.'

'How did he know about us? I didn't tell him,' she said.

'How do I know? Could your mother have said anything?' I asked.

'Doubt it. I haven't seen Peter. I can't imagine Mum speaking to him.'

'Doesn't matter,' I said and rang off. I wasn't in the mood to chat to neurotic women.


I phoned Jim Muriston at the *Glasgow Clarion*. There had been no fresh news from Maryhill.

That afternoon there was a magazine staff meeting to discuss the proposed contents of the next issue. As usual, I chaired the meeting, and it just felt so good. This was *me* again. I wish I still was.

The meeting ended at three. I spent the next couple of hours writing an article about Kevin Previn, a novelist from Glasgow whose private life was more interesting than his pot-boiling books. I'd decided to leave the feature about the happenings in Maryhill until the last minute. For the time being, I just didn't want to think about the place.

At five, I gave Ian a lift home. 'How d'you feel about

Friday night now?' he asked as I drove.

'Funny. I know it can't have happened, and when I think about it I don't believe it did. But I can't explain it. I can't explain how whoever it was on the phone knew what he knew. It's something I've never mentioned to anybody.'

Ian looked at me curiously. 'Want to tell me?'

I shook my head. 'Nah. In fact, I don't really want to talk about any of it. I'm feeling a lot better now. I just want to put it to the back of my mind for a while.'

'Okay.'

'I'll tell you about it sometime.'

'When you're ready. So, how's it with you and Trish?' he asked, changing the subject. 'You seem happier.'

'Uh-huh. It's going well. Though just over a week ago I thought it was going to finish. It's just picked up. Weird!' I laughed.

'No weirder than anything else recently,' he said.

I dropped him off outside his flat, declining his invitation to come in. Then I headed home.

Trish was curled up on the sofa reading. She looked up and smiled as I came in. 'Hi,' she said.

'Hi.' I took off my jacket and hung it by the door. 'How're you?'

She put down her book, stretched and said, 'I'd a really nice day. How about yours?'

'Great.' I sat down beside her and gave her a shove. 'Move over.' She did, and I stretched out on the sofa and put my arms around her. She kissed me on the nose and snuggled against me. 'You know, I really could get used to having you around here,' I told her.

'Mm. So could I,' she murmured, snuggling closer.

'What?'

'So could I.'

'Are you serious?' I demanded.

'Yes.'

'But I've been asking you to move in for more than a year. You keep saying you couldn't put up with me.'

'So ask me now.' She kissed me again.

'Fancy moving in with me for good?'

'Yes, please.'

Later that night, we were lying in bed, and I asked her, 'What brought on the change of heart?'

'Don't know.' She stroked my hair. 'I've felt really different lately. I don't know why.' She was quiet for a moment. 'Last night probably decided me. I had this really horrible dream about you. When I woke up and saw you lying there I just wanted to hold you.'

'What was the dream?' I asked.

'Never mind. It'd give you the heebies.'

'Come on, that's not fair! Tell me or I'll tickle your feet,' I threatened.

She giggled. 'Okay. It was *horrible*. You were in this street. I didn't recognise it but it looked like Maryhill. There was this woman standing looking at you. She had magnets instead of hands and –'

Chilly fingers ran over my scrotum.

'She was pulling you towards her. You were screaming for me to help you.'

'And?' I sounded strangled but Trish didn't notice.

'Then I woke up.'

111

For a second I wondered if I'd told Trish about the dream about my mother, knowing that I hadn't. Then I got out of bed.

'Where're you going?'

'To see Ian,' I lied. 'What you said just reminded me of something. Something urgent. I have to see him.'

'I don't believe you,' she said, voice shrill.

I put the light on (*It's dark here, Gary*) and began to dress.

I'd been sitting in my car outside the Bogey Close for an hour. I'd seen and heard nothing. I didn't know why I'd driven up there, only that I'd had to.

For an hour I'd sat staring at the dark mouth of the close, watching for (*my mother*) the Bogey Man. But really, I knew I wasn't going to hear that chant again. You didn't hear it if you wanted to. We knew that as kids.

I started the car — and, if it wasn't bizarre enough already, here it becomes totally fantastic. I looked at the dashboard, and my first reaction was to laugh out loud at the horror film cliché I saw there. Then I stopped laughing.

The car milometer read 000666.

Whimpering to myself, I tore my eyes away from it to look at the road. I was out of Hunterdunn Street and halfway down Maryhill Road before I looked at the milometer again. The reading was normal.

I drove to Ian's flat in the Merchant City. It was one in the morning but he was still up, watching a video. 'I thought you'd appear,' he said as he opened the door.

'I've had Trish on the blower twice. She said you started acting weird. Told her you were coming to see me.'

'That's right. I lied,' I said as I followed him into the living room. 'I wasn't planning to come here at all.'

'So what brought you?' he asked.

I started to tell him, but he cut me off. 'Wait a minute. I'm going to phone Trish and tell her you're here.' He picked up the phone. 'Go and make us some coffee,' he suggested.

'Right.' I went to his kitchen, put the kettle on and made coffee for Ian and tea for myself. As I did, I heard him talking to Trish on the phone.

'Hi, it's Ian. Just to let you know, Gary's here. A couple of minutes ago. No, he's in the kitchen. I will, don't worry. Well, he seems okay. Don't worry. Bye.'

I went into the living room and handed him his mug. He was sitting in one of two deep armchairs by the gas fire. It was a warm, *normal* room, the sort of living room you'd expect a guy older than Ian to have. I never wanted to leave it now.

Ian sat in silence as I told him what had happened that night. When I'd finished he just looked at me. 'So?'

'So,' I said, 'I want you to come up there with me tonight and see if it happens again.'

He shook his head. 'No chance. It's impossible. It's mad, and I'm not going to be mad enough to go along with it.'

'You think I've flipped now?' I demanded

'Yes. I do,' he admitted. 'I think you should see a doctor.'

113

'Look, if I'm nuts, come with me and show me I'm nuts. If I see it and you don't, then at least I'll know.'

'Tell me now,' said Ian, face grey in the light of the streetlamps. 'Is this a fucking joke, Gary?' We were sitting in my car outside the Bogey Close in Hunterdunn Street. The car engine was running, the dashboard lit up. The milometer read 000666

'No, it's not.' Now I knew, now I knew it was happening, I felt more afraid than when my own sanity had been in question.

'What *is* it? What's it doing?'

'I haven't a clue.' My glasses were steamed with my sweat. I took them off and wiped them. 'Jesus.'

'What do we do?' asked Ian.

I looked over to the Bogey Close. 'We get out of here.' I pulled away from the kerb and was heading out of Hunterdunn Street when I knew what I had to do.

'What's going on?' said Ian, as I did a U-turn and headed back to the Bogey Close.

'I want to check something out,' I told him.

'Fuck that. Let's get away from here!'

'My sentiments too, but this'll only take a minute.' I parked, training the headlights on the Bogey Close. 'I'm going in there —' I began.

'I'm not,' Ian said

'I don't want you to. I want you to sit here in the driver's seat and make sure, whatever happens, that the headlights stay on that close. Keep the engine going, and when I get back to the car, just get us away from here. No questions till we're back at your place. Right?'

Ian nodded. I got out of the car and he moved into the driver's seat. In a voice of a child I said, 'Whatever happens, don't leave me. Please.'

Ian didn't answer. I walked towards the Bogey Close.

The blackness in the close was like a solid wall. The headlights didn't penetrate it at all. When I got right up to the entrance to the close, I looked over my shoulder at the car. I couldn't see anthing but the glare of the headlights, illuminating me, the wall around the close, but making no impression on the blackness within.

Was I really going in there? The darkness actually looked so solid that I'd bump into it. I clenched my teeth.

*'It's dark here, Gary,'* said a voice from the blackness, and I felt my bladder give way. *'Wet yourself, Gary? Tut, tut. Your mummy won't be pleased. She's in here, you know. Come on in and see her.'*

I looked at the puddle of urine on the ground at my feet. 'Oh, Jesus.'

*'Jesus? No, he's not in here. Too dark for him. But we've got lots of people you know.'*

There was a moment of silence, then Glenn Lenzie's voice said, *'Hi, boss. Want to see my new article? You won't like it, Mr Fucking Cuntface Editor. But I'm going to hold out this time. Want to see how I hold out? You did ask. Come on in and I'll show you. Come on.'*

I began to cry.

*'Stop fucking blubbering, boss. Doesn't suit you,'* the Lenzie-thing said. *'Hey, guess who else is in here? Your little Yid. Come in and see her.'*

A second later, Rhona's voice pleaded, *'Gary, come in*

*and help me. Peter's going to break my other arm.'* And I knew that somehow, that day, Rhona had been killed.

Then came the one thing I could never, ever, face. A woman's voice I know horribly well said, *'Gary Scott! Wet yourself again! Mummy'll have to burn you. It breaks my heart. Don't you love your mummy, you dirty little fucker?'*

'Mum –' I started to moan, and then, taking in what was happening, I clutched my stomach and began to shriek.

*'Quiet!'* my mother's voice went on *'– what a noise! Mummy'll have to give you a good burning. Did you think Mummy couldn't burn you any more – just because she's fucking dead?'*

From somewhere far away I heard Ian call my name, then I was running towards the car, crying and swearing and trembling, feeling my piss-soaked jeans clinging to my legs. 'Get us the fuck out of here!' I screamed at him, and he drove off as soon as I was in my seat.

Ian slowed down as we reached Maryhill Road. 'Look at the milometer,' he told me. It still read 000666.

'What happened back there?' Ian asked.

'Never mind. You wouldn't believe it anyway.'

'After this, I'd believe anything,' he said. 'You've wet yourself, haven't you?'

'I'd noticed,' I answered. 'It's a wonder I didn't shit myself too. Come on, get us home.'

Ian speeded the car up and we headed down Maryhill Road. The milometer reading didn't change. We'd gone about two hundred yards when I saw a van parked at the side of the otherwise deserted road. Its back door was open, and in the couple of seconds it took us to pass the van I could see in.

Inside the van there was a small square table, surrounded by stools. At the table sat Glenn Lenzie, Rhona Jacobs, Lesley Tobin and a little girl I knew was Clare Gibney. As we passed the van, they all smiled and waved to me.

I buried my head in Ian's lap, almost causing him to crash. 'What's up?' he said, shocked. The van had been on the left side, my side, of the car, and Ian hadn't seen the occupants.

'That van! That van! Is it following us?'

'No, it hasn't moved,' said Ian. 'Why? What's wrong?'

'It was full of dead people, Glenn Lenzie included,' I said, sitting up again.

'I'll tell you what really worries me,' said Ian. 'What worries me is the fact that I don't disbelieve you.'

'Look,' I said, pointing. The milometer reading was now normal.

# TEN

I removed my stinking jeans and put them in the washbasket as soon as I got into my flat. I undressed in the living room, washed, then crept to the bedroom, hoping not to wake Trish. I had phoned her from Ian's after I'd persuaded him to come to Maryhill. I told her Ian and I had a few things to do, and not to worry. I hoped she hadn't.

She was still awake when I got into bed with her. Without a word she hugged my naked body to hers. 'Mm. That's what I said I could get used to,' I said, stroking her hair.

'Where were you?' she asked.

'Top secret. Magazine business. I can't tell you yet,' I said lightly.

'I thought you were seeing somebody else,' she said.

'What?'

'When you left like that tonight, I thought maybe you had somebody else,' she said, holding me tighter. 'That's why I phoned Ian to see if you were there. I'm sorry for checking up on you.'

I kissed her. 'D'you think I'd ask you to move in with me, then head off to fuck someone else?' I asked.

'I don't know. You've been acting so weird, I almost hoped that's what it was.'

119

'No more weirdness,' I promised. 'It'll be over soon.'

Trish looked at the clock on the bedside table. 'God, four in the morning. I'm knackered.'

'Haven't you slept?' I asked.

'No. Some idiot stood under the window singing all night. He just kept singing this same stupid kids's song, like a nursery rhyme.'

*It's dark here. Gary.*

'D'you remember it?' I asked, trying to sound casual.

'He sang it so many times I know it by heart,' she said. *'I'm the Bogey, Bogey, I'm the Bogey Man. I'm there when it gets dark, to kill you if I can.* Like something you'd sing to frighten a kid.'

'Uh-huh. Go to sleep.' I felt totally calm. After what'd happened that night, it was going to take a lot to upset me. So I'd just had the Bogey Man outside my window singing to Trish for a few hours. No problem to our hero.

I lay awake, tried to think and couldn't. I'd dropped Ian off at his flat, telling him we'd have a talk about what had happened when we met at the office. I hoped he'd have some ideas, but knew he wouldn't. I knew nobody could understand what was going on as well as I could, and I didn't understand it at all.

As I dropped off to sleep, I knew what I had to do. I would phone Mark Allen in Edinburgh and agree that we should set up a magazine together. Mark and I would have different ideas, but if I pushed him, I could probably make the magazine another, perhaps even better, version of the *City Review*. Trish and I would move to Edinburgh. She'd be able to get work there easily enough. She was a good teacher, her CV was strong. Why not? We could settle together and forget Maryhill ever existed.

Maybe.

I got up at six-thirty, having slept for only about an hour. Trish didn't wake. I had a shower, then a breakfast of toast and oranges. I knew I must eat, but I couldn't stomach anything heavier. Then I went out for a *Glasgow Clarion* to see if there was anything about Rhona. I had no doubt at all that she was dead.

I was right. The report was on page two. She'd been stabbed to death by Peter, who was now in custody. I didn't read any more. I didn't have to.

I'd been reading the paper as I walked back to my flat from the shop. As I reached my close, I tore it in two and stuffed it into a wastebin.

Before I left the flat at eight-forty-five, I woke Trish. 'If you go to work now, you'll be late,' I said. 'You'd be best having the day off.'

'I shouldn't.' She yawned. She always looked her best in the mornings, and on this particular morning she looked lovelier than I'd ever seen her. 'You should've wakened me earlier.'

'I didn't want to. I knew you were tired.' I put my jacket on.

She smiled. 'Well, if I'm having the day off, you should at least be late.'

'What d'you mean?'

'I mean come back to bed and make love to me.'

I know what you'll think of me and I don't blame

121

you for thinking it, but, in spite of just having discovered the death of a girl I'd slept with only about a week before, I did just as Trish said. And was glad to. I just wanted to curl up inside her and stay there.

I left her an hour later. My phone had rung twice and I'd ignored it. Trish was lying in bed, lightly dozing, when I bent over her and kissed her forehead. Without opening her eyes, she smiled, reached up to slip her arms around my neck, pulled me down and kissed me. 'I think I'm in love.' She sighed.

'Seriously?' I said sharply.

'Mm-hm.' She opened her eyes and looked at me.

'I take it it's me you're in love with?'

She grinned and shook her head. 'No, you prat. Your bum.' She threw a pillow at me as I headed for the door.

'I love you,' I told her.

'Love you,' she said.

'You're still a pain in the arse.'

'So're you.'

'Love me anyway?' I asked.

'Uh-huh. Go to work before I have you back in bed,' she said. I went.

It was a quarter to eleven when I got into my office. Ian was sitting at my desk. He looked drawn and hadn't shaved. 'Rhona's dead,' he said as soon as I came in. 'She's been murdered.'

'I know. I knew she was dead last night.'

'How?' He looked at me as though I'd had a hand in killing her, which, in a funny sort of way, I suppose I had.

'Remember I told you what I saw in that van we passed last night?'

'Yes.'

'Rhona was one of the people in it.'

Ian rubbed his face with his hands. 'Shit. I was sort of hoping you'd come in here and not know what I was talking about when I mentioned last night. Stupid, I know. But when I got in here this morning, everything seemed like it always does ...' He broke off, stuck for the words.

'I know exactly what you mean. I've been feeling like that for the past week.'

'I'll tell you something horrible,' Ian said. 'Rhona's just been murdered, and I don't care. Can you imagine that?'

'Snap,' I said. 'You've got an excuse; you didn't really know her. I slept with her, Ian. Now she's dead and I don't feel a thing.'

We sat and stared at each other. 'Gary, what are we going to do?' he finally asked.

'I don't know. I don't think there's anything we can do. Except what I'm going to do.'

'Which is?'

'Get out of Glasgow. Move to Edinburgh. Maybe it won't be able to reach me there. Maybe it can't reach that far.'

'What about —' He spread his hands. 'This place. The mag.'

'I don't really care, Ian. I only care about the voices I heard in that close last night. I know that whatever's up there wants to kill me. Sorry to be a coward, but I'm getting away before it does.'

The phone rang. 'Hello, Gary?' Heather said when I answered it. 'The police are here to see you.'

'Right. Tell them to wait a minute.' I put the phone down and looked at Ian. 'The police want to talk to me.'

'Oh, right.' Ian nodded. 'It's about your run-in with that boyfriend of Rhona's yesterday. They just want to know what happened. They were here earlier. They phoned your flat a couple of times, but got no answer.'

'Can you tell them to come through?' I said.

Ian nodded. He got up from my chair and suddenly hugged me. 'You're no coward, Gary Scott.' He was crying.

A moment after Ian left there was a knock on the door and two policemen came in. One of them was Pinky. 'Hi. How's Perky – I mean, Constable Jamieson?' I asked.

'Don't know. He quit the job,' said Pinky. 'He's gone to London. Just couldn't take it.'

I sat in my chair and looked at Pinky. He obviously didn't like Perky. He was about my age, brash and arrogant, and probably despised what he saw as Perky's cowardice. He was of the type that makes a good soldier, too stupid to know when to be afraid. He would probably die in Maryhill before very long.

'How's the investigation going?' I asked.

'It's not really me that's handling it,' Pinky told me. 'As far as I know, they're no further forward.'

They stayed about ten minutes, taking down my description of Peter's visit to the office. It appeared, they told me, that he'd gone straight from the office to Rhona's. She'd let him in, they'd quarrelled, and, in front of her mother, he'd grabbed a kitchen knife and stabbed Rhona more than a hundred times.

He told the police that the Bogey Man had made him do it.

# ELEVEN

Just before lunchtime, my phone rang. 'Someone called Sheena Watt on the blower for you,' said Heather. 'Says she's your neighbour.'

'Put her on.' Sheena lived upstairs from me. I really only knew her to say hello to. How she knew my number or why she might call it was a mystery.

'Hello, Gary. It's Sheena. From upstairs.'

'I know. What's up?'

'I've got some bad news, I'm afraid.'

I suddenly had an urge to scream. I could feel panic rising within me like vomit. I fought to control it, and won. 'What?' I croaked.

'Your girlfriend knocked on my door about an hour ago. She said she felt ill, and she looked terrible. I phoned an ambulance, and she passed out before it arrived.'

'Trish! Is Trish dead?' I felt as though I had my fingers in my ears, I could hear my blood pounding and my chest felt tight.

'No, she's not. Calm down.'

'Okay.' Please God Please God don't let her don't let her die –

'Are you all right?'

127

'Yes. What about Trish?'

'They took her to the Southern General. I don't know how she is. I got your number from a copy of your magazine.'

'What ward's she in?'

'25B.'


'She's in a diabetic coma,' the doctor said. 'She obviously didn't take her insulin.'

I just looked at him. We were in his office at the Southern General hospital. The office smelled of disinfectant and he smelled of mints. 'What d'you mean, insulin? She's not diabetic.' I spoke slowly, stupidly.

The doctor was one of those smart, obnoxious bastards who knows everything about bodies and nothing about people. 'Then she's doing a fine impersonation of someone in a diabetic coma,' he told me.

'But how d'you know it's a diabetic coma?' I asked.

'Blood tests, Mr Scott. The girl's seriously ill. She must have been on insulin. A day without it and she'd be dead. And she didn't develop such a severe condition in a day.'

'What can you do about – you know, the coma?'

'Just wait and hope she comes out of it,' he said.

Trish was in a room of her own. They had her wired and connected to God knows what. My bit of local infamy, plus the fact that Trish had no family so I was closest to next of kin they'd find, carried some weight, and they let me stay as long as I liked.

At ten that night, I was still there. A nurse came in to

check on Trish, and to ask if I wouldn't rather go home. When I said I'd rather stay if it was all right, she went and brought me some tea and biscuits.

I knew it was dark outside. I sat holding Trish's hand. She looked as though she might at any moment open her eyes, smile, and say that she loved me. I wondered if the dark would bring anything to try to harm her further. How, I wondered, did it get her during the day, out of Maryhill?

I had no doubt that something had got her. I knew that in theory it was possible that Trish could have been diabetic for years and, for whatever reason, kept it from me. But I also knew it wasn't true. And, even if it were true, Trish would never have forgotten to take her insulin. And she had told Sheena that she felt ill, not that she was diabetic and had no insulin.

Weren't people in comas supposed to be able to hear you sometimes? I began to mumble to Trish.

'Don't like seeing you like this, you know. I know you shouldn't be like this. I know something hurt you. But I'm not going to let it hurt you again, I promise.

'I love you, know that? I just want you to get better and we'll go away. D'you fancy going to live in Edinburgh? Ian said what about the mag, but the mag doesn't matter. When I got the mag going I was so proud of it. Remember how I used it to impress you when I met you at that party? It worked too. But the mag doesn't matter that much. I thought it did. But I don't care if I can't have the mag. I don't really want the mag that much. I don't really want anything. I don't care what I can't have, as long as I can have you.

'Pathetic, aren't I? I don't like being slushy. But I love you.' I was crying now. 'We've been really rotten to each other sometimes. But I'm not going to be any more. And I'm not going to let you get hurt like this again.

'I'd be so scared if you left me. I wouldn't have anybody. I wouldn't want anybody else anyway. Just want you.'

I continued to ramble till about three in the morning. The nurse brought me more tea from time to time. 'Mr Scott, I really think I should kick you out of here for your own good,' she said kindly. 'You look done in. Why don't you go home and get some sleep and come back later?'

'Okay.' I nodded. 'Just a few more minutes.' She went out. I bent over and kissed Trish. 'You take it easy, right? I really love you. I'm going home for a sleep. It's not fair you getting all the sleep. I'll be back soon. I love you.'

The nurse promised to phone me as soon as there was any change in Trish's condition. I drove to my flat. The sun was rising and the city was beautiful, and that made me want to throw up.

Five minutes after I'd arrived at my flat, the hospital phoned to tell me that Trish had died shortly after I'd left.

I don't suppose I need bother to describe my reaction. I'll just say my flat's in quite a state and leave it at that. I know I've got nothing now.

At half-five, I sat at my typewriter and started to write.

It's now ten-thirty in the evening. I've said all I've got to say. Except, as I suppose you're wondering, what next?

I'm going out to post this to the mag. I'll pick it up first thing on Thursday morning, assuming I'm there. You see, I'm going up to the Bogey Close tonight.

I could go off to Edinburgh. But, if it wants me, why couldn't it get me there? Or I could just sit here and wait for it to come. But I'm going to the Bogey Close, and I'm going to walk into that darkness and see what happens. Maybe nothing will. Maybe it can't hurt you if you face it. Maybe that's why it didn't kill me on Monday night.

Or maybe I'm mad. Whatever, I'll soon know. But if other people're to die, I should be next. Because I've a feeling that, somehow, I'm the cause of it all.

*It's dark here.*

*There's no light.*

# A NOTE ON THE AUTHOR

Barry Graham was born in Glasgow and is in his early twenties. He has had a variety of occupations, including professional boxing and journalism, and for a year was deputy editor of Glasgow's *Inside Out* magazine. In 1988 he moved to Edinburgh, where he is currently working on a second novel.